PRISCILLA SHIRER
WITH GINA DETWILER

PUBLISHING GROUP
Nashville,
Tennessee

Illustrations by Jon Davis.

978-1-4336-9019-8

Published by B&H Publishing Group
Nashville, Tennessee

Dewey Decimal Classification: JF
Subject Heading: BIBLE. N.T. EPHESIANS 6:10-18 /
SPIRITUAL WARFARE—FICTION

7 8 9 10 11 12 • 21 20 19 18 17

For Jackson
Our firstborn son.
Our Prince Warrior.

The Prince Warriors series

Book 1
The Prince Warriors

Book 2
The Prince Warriors and the Unseen Invasion

Book 3
The Prince Warriors and the Swords of Rhema

Unseen: The Prince Warriors 365 Devotional

Contents

PART ONE

Welcome to the Real World

CHAPTER ONE

Jumping In

There was something strange about that pond. Evan knew it from the first time he looked into its murky depths. What was down there? A monster? Like that one in Scotland, what was it called—Lock Ness? Something weird like that. He stood still, shivering a little, waiting for whatever it was to break through the surface and eat him. Alive. One gulp. He hoped it would be one gulp. He couldn't stand the thought of being chewed.

He was small enough for one gulp anyway. Not like his big brother, Xavier. Big, tough Xavier. With the cool name. Xavier even had muscles and armpit hair. Evan looked down at his own skinny, hairless arms. Not a muscle to be seen. No matter how many pull-ups he did from the tree branch of the big old oak in the back-yard, they just refused to grow.

"Going in today?"

Evan turned and saw his brother standing on top of the old tire that hung from one of the oak tree's thick branches. The tire had come with the tree, which had come with the house.

"Gonna do it today?" Xavier's face was all know-it-all-ish, as usual, the corner of his mouth turned up in a smirk.

Ever since they moved to this house from the city two months ago, Evan had stood on this little dock and stared at this pond, waiting for the day when he would get up the nerve to jump. Show Xavier he wasn't afraid. He had vowed to do it before the end of the summer, before starting fourth grade at his new school. He was sure by then he would have jumped in a hundred times. Yet here he was, a week before school opened, and he still hadn't done it even once.

And every single day, while Evan stood there shivering, Xavier would appear and rub it in.

"Want me to give you a push?" Xavier's grin got even wider.

"Go away," said Evan, teeth and fists clenched. He turned back to face the pond. *Jump! Jump!* But the encouraging voices in his head were drowned out by his brother's louder jibes.

"Come on, it's easy." Xavier jumped off the tire and sauntered up onto the dock, next to Evan. He was four inches taller. Sometimes it felt to Evan like four feet. "Watch me."

Xavier took a running leap and cannonballed like an Olympic diver, letting out a big whoop. Evan took a step back to avoid the gigantic splash.

"Go away!" he shouted.

"Come on, chicken," Xavier said, swimming to the dock and pulling himself up. "Just do it." He reached out to grab Evan, who pushed him away angrily.

"Leave me alone!"

"Chicken!" Xavier laughed again. "Chicken! *Cluck cluck cluck!*" He made some awful chicken noises and did a goofy chicken dance. Evan hated that dance. Xavier looked ridiculous doing it, but it always had the effect he wanted—to make Evan angrier than ever. Evan turned, red-faced, slamming into his big brother so hard the two of them went tumbling off the side of the dock, into the slimy mud at the edge of the water. *One punch,* Evan thought. *Just let me land one punch, and I'll be happy.* The voice in his head was louder this time.

"Boys!" their mom called from the porch. She'd been watching them, of course. Evan thought it actually might be true what she always said: that she had eyes in the back of her head. "What's going on?"

"I didn't do anything!" Xavier yelled back before Evan could find his voice. "I was trying to help him jump—"

"You're lying!" Evan's whole body shook with rage. He threw another punch, missing his brother by a foot.

"Evan! Come inside this house right now!" Mom's voice was all shriek-y. Bad sign.

Evan pushed away from Xavier and stood up. He was covered in mud. His face felt hot, like there was a fire creeping up the back of his neck. Xavier got up too, wiping mud off his shoulders, laughter still in his eyes.

"Evan!" Mom called. "March!"

"Chicken," Xavier whispered. Evan stifled the urge to cry and stomped into the house.

———

Xavier watched his little brother walk away. He felt sort of bad. He knew Evan was scared of jumping into the pond. He could have helped him. But every time he tried, it just came out wrong. He thought teasing him would make him mad enough to do it. But it didn't work. Nothing he did ever worked. *I guess this is just the way it is between us,* he thought. *We'll be enemies forever.*

He used to love being Evan's big brother, taking care of him, making sure he didn't get into trouble. Once, when Evan was still a baby, Xavier picked him up out of the crib, holding him upside down by his legs, and carried him into the bedroom where his mom and dad were sleeping. *Look!* he said so proudly. *I got Van!* His mom sort of freaked out, he remembered. His dad laughed.

Lately, though, all they seemed to do was fight. Evan got mad at the littlest things. Xavier figured his little brother was just jealous since Xavier was bigger and better at pretty much everything. He *was* four years older, after all. So what if he had a phone? *And* got to stay up an hour later? *And* was always picked first for the basketball games at the Rec? That's just the way things were.

After a while Xavier went into the house, where his mother had just finished reading Evan the Riot Act. That's what she called it. *The Riot Act.* What was the Riot Act anyway? He'd have to look that up. He liked looking up stuff. Whenever he asked his dad a question, his dad would say, "Look it up," which Xavier used to think meant, "I have no idea." But as he got older, he realized his dad knew there were some things he just had to figure out for himself.

Evan was sent to his room until supper. Then early bedtime. No basketball at the Rec tonight. Xavier felt a little bit bad. He should have gone into the kitchen and told his mom what he did to provoke Evan. Instead, he went into his room and searched on his phone:

Riot Act.

A few entries popped up.

Established in 1714 by the British Government. An act for preventing tumults and riotous assemblies . . .

What's a tumult? Xavier looked it up. *Chaos.* So, the Riot Act was for punishing people who caused chaos. Okay, that made sense. Sort of. Did it work? Xavier scanned the rest of the entry. From what he saw, apparently not. He figured you just couldn't write a rule outlawing chaos and expect everyone to follow it.

"Xavier! Come set the table!" Mom called from the kitchen. Suppertime. Dad would be home soon.

Xavier stuffed the phone in his pocket and went down to the kitchen. He loved the phone—he'd only gotten it when they moved to this house from the city a couple of months ago. Xavier thought it might have been a bribe for having to leave his old neighborhood. But he was also told he had to share the phone with his little brother. Share a phone with a nine-year-old? Where did parents get these ideas? Some clueless parenting handbook?

"Set the table," Mom said as soon as he set foot in the kitchen. She turned away from him to pull something from the oven.

"It's Evan's turn," Xavier said.

"You boys are so good at remembering whose turn it is, aren't you?" Her voice was sharper than usual. "Just do it, please. I don't have time to argue."

I don't have time to argue. Another one of Mom's favorite sayings. Who didn't have time to argue? That just didn't make sense. Xavier considered arguing to be one of the most important skills of life. He thought he might even be a lawyer when he grew up. Or a professional basketball player. He hadn't quite decided.

He set the table. Dad came in with his briefcase, kissed Mom on the cheek, and put his hand on Xavier's shoulder. "So, kiddo, how was your day?"

I got Evan in trouble, Xavier thought. But he said, "Pretty good."

"Just pretty good?"

Xavier shrugged. "Played ball at the Rec. Mr. J. Ar says I've got *potential.*" That was the word Mr. J. Ar had used. *Potential.* Xavier liked it. "There's another pickup game tonight. Can I go?"

"Don't see why not. Where's Evan?"

"In his room," Mom said, "having a cool-off period." (Mom's word for *time-out*.) "Fighting again."

"It takes two to fight, doesn't it?" said Dad, looking suspiciously at Xavier.

"I didn't do anything!" Xavier said, shrugging in the most innocent way he could. "He's just mad because he's still afraid to jump in the pond. So he takes it out on me."

"He'll do it when he's ready," Mom said. "Did you pour the water into the glasses on the table yet?"

Xavier poured the ice-cold water and helped Mom put forks and stuff on the table. He was on his best behavior now. *I'm the good son.*

"All set for school starting next week?" Dad asked, stealing a green bean from a bowl on the counter.

"Sure, I guess," said Xavier. He had tried to avoid thinking about school—a new school in a new town, a whole new group of kids—although he didn't want his dad to think he was scared or anything. He wasn't scared, exactly. He was already pretty popular at the Rec, after all. He was good at sports, which was the main thing. But he always wondered, in the back of his mind, if he was really good *enough*.

Xavier glanced up to see his dad peering at him curiously, as if he could read his thoughts. He gave him a lopsided grin. "Don't worry, Dad. It'll be cool." His dad smiled back.

CHAPTER TWO

A for Ahoratos

Levi put the finishing touches on his drawing—he needed to get the details right. He should know it by heart by now. He'd seen it often enough in his dreams— the strange symbol shaped a little bit like a squiggly *N* or *X*, depending on how you looked at it. He woke up every morning with the image burned into his mind.

Ahoratos. The name whispered in his head over and over.

What was it? What did it mean? And why was it haunting him?

He sat on a bench against the wall of the Cedar Creek Recreational Center, facing the skateboard park, his board at his side. His friends were all out skating, practicing new tricks. Across the parking lot, other kids were gathering for a game of basketball. Levi glanced over and saw that new kid Xavier trotting out onto the court, hands in the air, laughing. Xavier had quickly become King of Basketball at the Rec. Or he seemed to think he was.

"Hey, Levi! Come show us something, man!" his friends called, beckoning him out onto the ramps.

"In a minute," he called back. He yawned. He loved skateboarding, but he was too tired at the moment. The dreams were starting to get to him.

Ahoratos . . .

The word seemed to float like a feather in his mind, wafting this way and that, always near but just out of his reach.

"What's up, Levi? Want to join in the pickup game?"

His dad's voice snapped him back to reality. He looked up to see his father towering over him, arms folded across his chest: James Arthur, known to the other kids as Mr. J. Ar. He wore a whistle around his neck, which meant he was going to ref the basketball game.

"No thanks," Levi said.

"What you got there?" His dad peered down at the sketchbook. Levi tilted it to his chest so his dad couldn't see. Levi still wasn't sure he wanted anyone to know he liked to draw. It didn't seem cool. Besides, his dad would want to know what that weird symbol was and why he was drawing it, and Levi didn't really have an answer for him anyway.

"Uh—nothing." He could feel his father's eyes boring little holes in the top of his head.

"Maybe next time then, okay?"

"Sure. Sounds good."

Levi watched him trot across the parking lot to the basketball court. That's what his dad did now: trot. He said college football had worn his knees down too much for real running. A crowd of kids followed him, as usual. All the kids loved Levi's dad. He spent many evenings at the Rec, even after a long day's work, volunteering his time so the kids would have a fun place to hang out. Good thing, too, because without him there, the place would be utter chaos. The only staff person was a part-time college student who spent most of her time in the office, studying for some summer course she was taking, drinking chai lattes from Starbucks, and texting her college friends. A squad of ninjas could rappel through the roof and she wouldn't know a thing about it.

"Levi!"

Brianna Turner suddenly stood in front of him, a tube of lip gloss in her hand as usual. She'd apparently just applied it because her lips looked like she'd kissed a bowl of glitter. She wore black-and-white striped leggings and a pink hoodie with sequins around the pockets, even though it was over eighty degrees. She stuffed the lip gloss into the hoodie pocket and flopped down next to him on the bench. Her lip gloss smelled like peaches.

"Hey, Bean," he said. He still called her that, even though he knew she didn't really like it anymore. He couldn't remember why he had come up with that nickname in the first place. Maybe because she was skinny like a string bean. Or maybe it was just easier to say than *Brianna*.

"Whatcha drawing?" Brianna leaned over to look. Her thick mass of long tight curls—barely held back by a wide sparkly headband—practically took out his eye.

"Nothin'." Levi tried to hide his sketchpad from her, but she grabbed it away from him.

"Is it a picture of *me*?" she chirped. Brianna always thought everything was about her.

"Hey!" Levi snatched the sketchpad back, but not before Brianna had caught a faint glimpse of the unfinished image he'd drawn.

"Wait . . . I've seen this before!" She squinted—that's what she did when she was deep in thought. Levi slowly turned the page back in her direction so she could look at it again. "This part is wrong." She grabbed his pencil and made an adjustment. "See? This is how it goes. Those little knobs are much wavier—"

"You've seen it?" Levi said, astonished. "When?"

She took a breath before speaking, as if she wasn't sure she wanted to tell him about it. "Last night. And the night before. And—most nights before that too."

Levi blinked, his mouth dropping open. "You saw it—like in a dream?"

"Yeah."

"Me too."

"Seriously?" Brianna whispered. She looked relieved that she wasn't the only one. "That's so weird! How come you never told me before?"

"How come you never told *me*?"

She shrugged. "'Cause I thought you'd think I was crazy."

"Same here."

Brianna—Bean—had been Levi's best friend for as long as he could remember. Even though at first she'd annoyed the heck out of him. She lived next door in a tiny house with her grandparents and three older sisters. When they were little, she never had anyone her age to play with, so she was always coming over to Levi's house, wanting to play with him. At first he let her, just because he felt sorry for her. But she would insist on doing things *her* way. Levi's mom said it was because she was the youngest of her sisters and didn't have anyone to boss at home.

It drove Levi crazy. Like when Brianna used to make his Avengers action figures have tea parties with her Barbie dolls. Thankfully she'd outgrown that now. But when they played Uno or Monopoly, she would make up her own set of rules and then change them whenever she felt like it. The worst was during kickball, when she would tell all the other team members what they were doing wrong, as if she were the coach. Good thing she didn't play much kickball anymore, because it might mess up her hair, which had become unbelievably important to her all of a sudden. Levi didn't get it.

Still, he was used to Brianna now. He liked to hear her tell stories. She read a lot, and she could make up her own stories about anything. Once, Levi asked her to tell him a story about a blade of grass, and she spouted off an epic adventure about a blade of grass that managed to avoid the lawn mower in all sorts of crazy ways. Brianna made him smile. Even if she *was* way too bossy.

"What do you think it is?" Levi asked her. He knew she'd have an opinion. She always did.

"It's called an *Alef.* It's kind of like the letter *A*, except in a different language."

"How did you know that?"

"Grandpa Tony gave me this old book awhile ago— it has that same symbol on the cover. I used to read the book all the time. I asked Grandpa what the symbol meant and he told me: *A* for *Ahoratos.*"

Ahoratos! It was the same word Levi heard in his dreams. Such a strange name, it couldn't be a coincidence. But she pronounced it A-HOR-a-tos, which sounded different from how he'd heard it: A-hor-A-tos. It was close enough. And, besides, her version was probably right anyway.

"What is it—Ahoratos?" Levi asked.

"It's the name of the kingdom in the book."

"Well, I never read that book. So why am I dreaming about it?"

"Maybe you did read it and you just don't remember. Or maybe I told you about it."

That was possible, Levi thought. Bean talked nonstop, and he didn't always listen.

"*Briaaaaannnna!* Where *are* you?" Shrieky girl voices emanated from inside the Rec. "You're supposed to be helping us!"

"I gotta go in," Brianna said, jumping up from the bench with a huge sigh. "They can't do a thing without me." She looked longingly out at the field, where a game of kickball had just started. She let out a breath and gave Levi a little shove. "Come on. Help us decorate for the dance party. We need someone tall to hang streamers."

"I don't do decorating, Bean. That's girl stuff. I'm going to skate some."

Her face clouded like she was deeply hurt. But honestly, he couldn't be seen hanging around with her so much, especially doing things like *decorating.*

"Fine. Be that way." She spun around and stalked off in a gigantic huff. He shrugged, stuffed his sketchpad in his backpack, grabbed his helmet and skateboard, and headed out to the skate park.

Mr. J. Ar and a few of the other dads had built the skate park next to the Rec so that kids would have a safe place to skate. It had ledges and ramps, a quarter pipe, and even a fun box, which was a big box with a bunch of ramps attached to it. A dozen kids were skating, practicing their ollies and kick flips. Most stopped to high-five Levi as he pumped over to his friends Jeff, Logan, and Mikey at the mini ramp.

"'Bout time," Jeff said. "Too busy talking to your girlfriend?"

"She's not my girlfriend," Levi said, annoyed. He bent down to check the laces on his brand-new Vans.

Black high-tops, with a gold swag on the side. He kind of wanted the other kids to notice them. He was always particular about his shoes, but these were the coolest he'd ever owned. He wasn't supposed to wear them— his mom didn't want him getting them scuffed up before school started—but he needed to break them in. Besides, they were just too awesome *not* to wear.

The skaters took turns on the quarter pipe, working on their kick turns and nose slides. Levi was about to do a run on the fun box when he heard commotion from inside the Rec. Noisy laughter and shouting. The other kids stopped riding and looked in that direction too.

"What's going on in there?" asked Mikey.

"Let's go see," said Levi. The skaters left their boards and hurried into the building. Levi went in first to see Brianna and the girls, still holding party decorations, huddled against the wall. Some of them looked scared, but some were laughing. He caught Brianna's eye—she was furious.

In the center of the room stood four big, menacing boys. They were laughing like hyenas at a white shape writhing around on the floor. It took Levi a few seconds to realize it was a kid—completely wrapped up in toilet paper.

"Look! It's a mummy!"

Levi glimpsed a pair of thick red glasses and a knot of dark hair peeking out from the paper wrapping. He sighed. *Manuel.* That dorky smart kid. He was always getting picked on.

Levi heard his skateboarder friends laughing along with the rest. Brianna glared at them, frowning. The main bully, whose name was Landon, bent over to speak to Manuel in a taunting, falsetto voice.

"He's crying! I think he misses his mummy!"

More raucous laughter. It was a cruel joke—Landon probably didn't even know that Manuel's mom died a year ago. Or maybe he did, and that's why he said it. He was just that mean. Manuel flailed on the floor, trying to free himself from the wrappings.

"Man, look at that baby," said Jeff, nudging Levi. "I think he's gonna start crying."

"Cut that out!" Brianna marched up to Landon and his crew with her fists balled up, all eighty pounds of her ready to explode. The bullies only laughed louder. Levi moved toward her, wanting to get her out of their line of fire. She brushed him off.

"Mind your own business, *princess*," Landon sneered, pushing her out of the way. Brianna almost fell, and Levi quelled an impulse to go and help her. She'd just be mad at him for treating her like some fragile doll. Brianna straightened, one hand going up to check that her headband was still in place.

The four boys continued to taunt Manuel, saying, "Hey, what's the matter, kid? Walk much?" and other stuff like that. Manuel stumbled around, trying to stand up.

Brianna stalked over to Levi, her brown eyes pulsing with fury. "You've got to help him!" she whispered hoarsely. Levi took a breath—what could he do anyway? He felt sorry for the kid, but he wasn't about to get a bloody nose over it, not in front of his friends.

Just then the office door flew open and Mary Stanton, the college student, burst in—a phone in one hand, a Starbucks cup in the other.

"What's going on here?" she demanded, clearly annoyed at being interrupted from her important texting. She took one look at Manuel and let out a gasp. "What are you kids *doing*?"

"Nothin', Miss Stanton," said Landon with mock innocence, trying to keep a straight face. The boys behind him continued to snicker. They didn't take the college student very seriously—she was certainly no match for four hefty boys.

"You need to get your dad!" Brianna hissed to Levi. "Miss Stanton can't handle this herself."

Brianna was right, and Levi knew it. Only Mr. J. Ar could deal with these boys.

Levi was about to turn and run out the door when something caught his eye. A flash, there and gone again, above Landon's head. Levi blinked, wondering what he was seeing. Before he could dismiss it, there it was again, a golden object a few inches wide, turning slowly in midair, catching the light. Then he realized what it was: the same symbol he had dreamed about nearly every night. The one he'd tried to draw earlier. Everything around him—the boys, the girls, the room—dimmed slightly in comparison to this amazing, incredible sight. It seemed to have its own spotlight. As he stared, his eyes glazed over, kind of like the way they did when he watched TV for too long.

"What's the matter with you?" Brianna asked, punching him on the shoulder.

"Can't you see it?" Levi muttered, pointing to the thing over Landon's head.

"See what?"

Brianna turned in the direction he was looking, and when she caught her breath, Levi knew she could see it too. He was secretly relieved. Glad to know he wasn't just making all this up in his head.

They both stared in silence, ignoring the commotion around them. There it was—that symbol. *A* for *Ahoratos*. Hovering in the air, shimmering as if bathed in some celestial light all its own. Yet no one else seemed aware of it. Only Levi and Brianna.

Levi's dad burst in. "What's going on in here?" His deep voice echoed through the room, jolting the duo out of their trance. The bullies backed off, and the laughter stopped. Big, barrel-chested Mr. J. Ar commanded everyone's attention.

He went over to help Manuel to his feet. Mary Stanton rushed in as well, eager to help now that the danger was averted for the moment.

"You okay, son?" Mr. J. Ar asked.

Manuel nodded, apparently too shaken up to speak. Mr. J. Ar handed him over to Miss Stanton, who helped unravel him enough for him to walk with her toward the office.

Mr. J. Ar's ferocious eyes turned to the four bullies. Levi got a little chill. He knew what it was like to have those eyes stare down at him when he'd done something wrong. His dad's eyes could be full of kindness, but push the wrong buttons and they'd bore a hole into your soul.

"Hey, we didn't hurt him." Landon looked defiantly into those intimidating eyes. He didn't seem to be afraid of Mr. J. Ar at all. That kid was braver—or dumber—than Levi thought.

"You boys go on home now." Mr. J. Ar didn't raise his voice—he didn't have to.

Landon held that iron-hard gaze a moment longer, then let out a laugh and sauntered toward the door, trailed by his friends. "Just having fun," he muttered as he went. The symbol went too, hovering over Landon's head, bigger and more real than ever.

"We need to get that thing!" Brianna whispered, pulling Levi toward the door.

"No, Bean, you're crazy." But he went anyway, still curious about the strange symbol and also nervous that Brianna might try to confront those boys again. She still needed protection, even if she didn't think so.

When they got outside the door, they saw that Landon had stopped at the water fountain for a drink. The symbol hovered over his head, still turning slowly, still glowing.

"Now's our chance! While he's not looking!" Brianna whispered. The other boys had continued walking, so Landon was alone for the moment.

"I'll do it," Levi said, stepping in front of her. "He'll just knock you flat." *He'll probably knock me flat, too, but at least I can take it better.* He casually walked to where Landon was bent over the fountain, acting as if he was just going to stand in line for a drink. Then, he reached above Landon's head toward the rotating object.

21

At that exact moment Landon straightened, knocking into Levi's arm. The kid whirled on him, his big face reddening.

"Hey, idiot! What's up with you?"

"Nothing," Levi said, smoothing his hand over his hair casually. "I just . . . saw this giant bug about to land on your head, so I was swatting it away."

"A bug?" Landon suddenly looked worried.

"Yeah, one of those big black things—what do you call them?"

"It was a black-horned Wolfwinger," Brianna said, in her I'm-way-smarter-than-you voice. "Also known as the *Lupinas Ala . . . Maribunta*. The worst kind. A stinger the size of a ballpoint pen. Usually they aim for the eyes, to shoot poison right into your brain."

Landon's eyes grew big, then small again. "You're just making that up," he said.

"Am not," Brianna retorted, perfectly serious. "Can't believe you've never seen one before. It's *Maribunta* season right now. Didn't you read the poster inside describing what to do in the event of a *Maribunta* bite?"

Levi tried to hide his grin. Brianna loved to tell stories. And apparently Landon believed her.

"What—?" Landon started. Then he waved her away, dismissing the idea. "No way—"

Levi shouted. "There it is again! Duck!"

Levi and Brianna faked a duck, but Landon went down almost to the concrete, covering his whole head in fear. This was the moment Levi was waiting for. He grabbed for the symbol. It was real all right, solid like stone, which surprised him because it looked transparent. See-through. He didn't have much time to think about it, though, because there was a strange, irresistible pulling sensation, as if he were being sucked up into the sky. Bean had grabbed his elbow, so she felt it too. She gasped. It seemed as though the whole world around them was spinning, twisting into a vortex, like water going down a drain. Levi had an impulse to let go, make it all stop, but he found he couldn't. Maybe he didn't really want to. It was scary—but he had to know what was going to happen next. The world around him was spinning so fast he couldn't catch his breath. He held tight to the weird *A* thing, Brianna clinging to his other arm.

"Leviiiiiiiii!" He could hear her voice, but it sounded far away, caught up in the wind. Everything—the Rec, the grass, the trees, Landon—swirled together in a maze of color and then disappeared altogether.

———

Landon peeked out from under his arms, searching for the horrible bugs with the deadly stingers. He didn't see any bugs, and he also didn't see those two kids either. Where'd they go? *Ran away,* he thought. Although he'd only been down there for a couple seconds. Strange. Either way, they were gone now. Scaredy cats. Made up that stupid story about big bugs. Maybe. Probably. Yeah. As if that would scare him. He straightened, glancing around to make sure no one had seen him crouched on the ground. He stuck out his chest and strode away. Next time he saw those two kids, he'd get 'em back for that.

Levi and Brianna stood together, staring around them in wonder. They couldn't see the weird letter *A* anymore. They couldn't see anything, for that matter.

"Where are we?" Brianna said.

"I have no idea," Levi answered. He looked around, trying to get his bearings. As far as he could see, there was nothing but white sand and red sky.

CHAPTER THREE

Imagining Dragons

Dinner was quiet. Evan didn't want to talk to anyone. He couldn't even look at his brother. Right after dinner he went to his room and did some major sulking. He'd been sent to bed early. No basketball at the Rec. For something that wasn't even his fault. Well, it wasn't *all* his fault anyway.

He picked up a book he'd been reading, one his dad had given him for Christmas last year. He hadn't really liked it at first because it seemed like an old book, and usually he found old books pretty boring. But this book wasn't boring at all. It was about a fierce warrior (who was also a prince, of course) who lived in a place called Ahoratos, a beautiful land of giant castles and tall mountains and fanciful creatures that were sometimes a little frightening. It was a good story, with lots of battles and sword fighting, which was perfect because these were the only kinds of stories Evan really liked to read. The Prince Warrior was constantly having to save his kingdom from these awful dragons who kept attacking and burning down his villages with their fire breath and stealing all the people's gold. Sometimes the Prince Warrior had to rescue the princesses, who were always getting themselves in one mess or another. Evan didn't really care much for that part.

He went to the closet and pulled out his pretend armor. He didn't want his big brother to know he still played with it. He put on the breastplate, the belt, the helmet. They were only plastic, and they were getting way too small for him. Plus they were old-fashioned. He wished he could get a newer, cooler set, like from *Star Wars* or *Thor*, but he wouldn't dare ask for that. Xavier would just make fun of him—even though Evan knew for a fact that Xavier still had the cape from a Batman costume he wore to a party in the sixth grade.

Evan picked up the wooden sword and shield—his grandpa had made them for him when Evan was six. The shield had his initial, *E*, emblazoned in gold right in the middle. He swung the sword while he danced around the room, fighting the imaginary dragon that had started to look an awful lot like his brother. Xavier the dragon! Evan the Prince Warrior! The Prince Warrior always won.

Prince Warrior: 1,116,437

Dragon: 0

Finally he got tired. He shoved the armor under his bed with all the other stuff he never bothered to put away and went to the bathroom to brush his teeth. He heard the door slam downstairs. Xavier was home from basketball. Evan quickly finished in the bathroom and went into his room to put on his pajamas, shutting the door tight. At least they didn't have to share a room anymore, the way they used to in their apartment in the city.

He crawled into bed with his book and flashlight to read under the covers. He could hear his brother using the bathroom and getting ready for bed. *Clean the toothpaste out of the sink,* he thought. Xavier never cleaned the sink. It was disgusting.

He waited for Xavier to come into his room, to tease him about missing basketball, about being afraid to jump off the dock, about, well . . . *anything.* There always seemed to be an excuse for Xavier to barge in and torment him. But nothing happened. Evan was sort of disappointed. Maybe Xavier didn't even think about him enough to come in and tease him anymore.

When the door finally did open, it was Mom who came in. Evan quickly switched off the flashlight and hid the book under the covers.

"Feeling any better?" she asked, sitting down beside him on the bed. She reached under the covers and pulled the book and flashlight out. She laid them on top of the covers next to Evan's pillow. She wasn't mad. Just wanted him to know that she knew. Always did. *She definitely has eyes in the back of her head,* Evan thought.

She waited for his answer to her question. Evan was in no mood for a Mom Talk. He looked away and pulled the covers up to his chin. He heard her sigh.

"Evan, I know you were mad at your brother, but you need to find some way to deal with it other than fighting. These skirmishes have to stop."

"What's a skirmish?"

"It's like a battle, only shorter. Evan, do you get what I'm saying?"

Evan didn't answer. He tried to turn over, but she grabbed his shoulder and pulled him back, forcing him to look at her.

"Yeah, I get what you're saying. I'll . . . try," Evan said sullenly. "No more squishes."

"Skirmishes."

"Right."

"Good." She smiled, kissed him on the forehead, and got up to leave.

"Mom?" Evan pulled down his covers. Mom turned to look at him.

"What is it, honey?"

"Do you think I'll ever be in a—*real* battle?"

Mom's mouth opened slightly, and her eyes flitted around the room like she didn't know quite what to say. Then she sort of smiled.

"Oh yes, baby," she said. "You already are."

"I am?" Evan sat up, alarmed. Mom came to sit beside him again.

"You and Xavier—"

"I'm not talking about a . . . skirmish or anything like that. I mean a *real* battle. With swords and stuff."

"Oh, this *is* a real battle, Evan. There's a sneaky, malicious enemy that you are always in a battle with— even now."

"Xavier?"

"No, it's not Xavier."

"Then who is it?"

"Someone who wants to remain hidden so that you'll forget he's even there. He'll do everything he can to make you feel like you will never win."

"Will I . . . win, I mean?"

Mom thought about this for a while. "It won't be easy," she said finally. "But just remember this, Evan: no matter what this enemy throws at you, you *always* have what you need to win. So you never have to be scared. Capeesh?"

She meant, "Do you understand?" Mom had lots of weird words for stuff.

"Capeesh," Evan said, agreeing even though he wasn't so sure he *did* understand. "But about this enemy . . ."

"We'll talk more tomorrow," Mom said, winking at him. "Sweet dreams, Evan love."

Once she'd kissed him good night again (she loved gooey kisses), Evan lay back and pulled the covers up to his chin once more. Thinking about real battles sort of scared him, even though his mom had said he didn't have to be scared. He peered outside at the silver moon peeking through the branches of the big old oak. The moon was huge, bigger than he'd ever seen. Full. He started to imagine himself in his shiny armor, a Prince Warrior, riding a white horse through the mist toward some big castle on the top of a high mountain. What a cool picture that would be. He thought about getting up, getting out his colored pencils, and drawing it. The moon, the tree, the mountain, Prince Evan on a white horse. He yawned. Maybe tomorrow.

His eyes closed . . .

———

"Get up!"

Evan sprang upright, his book and flashlight falling to the floor with a thud.

"What?" He rubbed his eyes, searching for the owner of the voice. Was it a voice? He couldn't be sure. The room was dark. Eerie shadows moved around him, shadows of the tree branches in the yard shifting under the full moon.

"Hurry!"

Yes, a voice—soft, whispery, yet loud at the same time—filling his whole head.

"Come!"

A shadow darted across the room. Not the tree branch shadow, but a *creature* sort of shadow. A raccoon? A cat? No, too big for that. But too small for a person. The shadow jumped into the windowsill. In the moonlight Evan could make out a flowing garment, like a robe. A purple robe. The shadow creature turned away, revealing a glowing symbol on its back—Evan's mouth opened and closed involuntarily.

The symbol was the same one that was on the cover of his book. The book about Ahoratos.

Who are you? he wanted to ask. But no words came out of his mouth. It wouldn't open at all now. He just stared. The creature's head swiveled around, but Evan could not make out a face in the hood—as if the hood were actually *empty.*

"Hurry! Before it's too late!"

"Too late . . ." Evan's words started working but each one seemed to take forever to come out. "For . . . what?"

Suddenly the bedroom door burst open, and Xavier stomped in.

"Evan, there was this thing in my room—"

Evan's eyes flicked to his brother, who wore a wide-eyed expression. He turned back to the creature sitting in the window. *So he sees it too. I'm not imagining it.* Very slowly, Evan lifted his arm until his finger pointed directly to the silhouette of the *thing* sitting on the sill.

He heard Xavier gasp. "What . . . is . . . it . . . ?" He was having the same trouble with words that Evan had.

The creature spoke impatiently. *"Prince Evan, Prince Xavier. Follow me! Quickly!"* And then it disappeared out the window. The *second-floor* window.

Evan glanced at his brother's frozen face. He looked like he'd seen a ghost. Maybe they both had. But Evan didn't think so. He was suddenly filled with curiosity. He had to know what that creature was and what the big hurry was all about.

Evan jumped out of bed and headed for the windowsill.

"Wait! What are you doing?" Xavier hissed at him.

"He said we had to go with him!" Evan replied. The curtains of the window blew riotously, as if a storm were brewing outside. Evan looked out, scanning the darkness. The creature was nowhere to be seen. But there was something else—something glowing in the night air. There it was again! The same symbol from the book. It was huge, transparent yet somehow solid, shimmering as it spun slowly, suspended in space.

He heard the voice again. *"Come!"*

"Evan, you can't jump—you'll break your legs!" Xavier had come up beside him. He saw it too—the weird glowing object hovering in the air. "What is . . . ?" His voice trailed off.

Maybe it's a dream, Evan thought. It had to be. In which case, what harm could it do to follow the shadow creature and see what would happen next?

"Let's go!" Evan said.

"Wait!" Xavier nearly shouted. But Evan ignored him. It was only a dream.

He jumped.

Evan only dropped down a few inches before his feet hit the ground. Weird. Then his feet started sinking into thick black muck. Mud maybe. But different. Sticky. More like . . . cake batter. He turned around to face the window he'd just jumped out of, but it wasn't there anymore. The whole house was gone. He looked up. Above him the sky was bright—*red*. Not a peaceful, sunset red. It was a bright, fiery red. Like the sun had bled its colors all over the universe. He looked to his right and left. All around him stood tall trees with large black leaves, so close together there didn't seem to be any light between them. The trees were growing—getting taller as he watched, thicker, sprouting black leaves, blocking out the red sky. They encircled him, like giant, hideous soldiers, closing in. He was completely surrounded.

He heard a squishy, goopy sound and turned to see his brother standing in the cake batter next to him. Evan was surprised to see fear in Xavier's wide eyes. He'd always thought Xavier wasn't afraid of anything.

They looked at each other, but neither spoke, all their combined emotions muddling together and making it hard to know what to think or do. The silence, for that brief moment, was deafening.

Then the purple-robed creature appeared before them, making them both nearly jump out of their skins.

"Follow me!" The creature plunged into the circle of thickening trees, its gait a sort of waddling glide, half-leaping, half-running, like a turkey trying to fly. As it went, the leaves of the trees changed from black to

vivid purple, dripping like fresh paint as if they had been stained by the creature's robe.

"We need to go that way," Evan said, indicating the purple leaves.

"But how? There's no path or anything."

This was true. Around them the huge black trees loomed, growing ever taller. The little splash of purple leaves seemed like their only hope.

"It said to follow. That's where it went. So, let's go!" Evan used all his strength to make his feet work, pulling them out of the cake batter-y muck to take a step forward. It wasn't as hard as he thought it would be. He took another step, heading for the splotch of purple in the dense wall of trees. He noticed the purple leaves beginning to tremble, as if stirred by a sudden wind. But as he got closer he realized they were actually *parting*, revealing a narrow pathway marked by more purple leaves. The creature appeared at the end of the purple trail, glowing as if from its own inner light, still moving quickly and yet somehow never quite out of sight.

Evan turned to Xavier. "Let's go! This way!"

"Coming!"

The two boys started to run toward the purple path, Evan leading the way for once. It was like running in molasses, like one of those dreams where someone is chasing you but you can't seem to get away. But once they started, it became easier. They found as they picked up speed their feet didn't sink anymore, like they were running on top of the mud, feeling the wet splashes up their pajama pant legs. Before them the purple leaves trembled and parted, leaning away from the path as if to welcome them and give them room to pass through. Evan thought they were actually waving to him, calling out: *This way, this way.* Up ahead, just barely visible, the little guy in the purple robe continued to zigzag through the trees, drenching the leaves in purpleness as he went, opening up the path for them to follow.

"Hey, wait up!" said Xavier. He was having trouble keeping up with Evan, which was definitely a new thing. Evan found he was starting to like this dream a tiny bit.

Then a loud rumble sounded overhead, stopping Evan in his tracks. *Was that thunder?* But the rumble didn't stop. It grew and grew, making the huge black trees around them quake as if with fear. Evan looked up at the sky, which was changing from bright red to purple-black, like a bad bruise.

Xavier caught up, panting. "What was that?" Evan didn't answer. He was too scared to speak. They heard a loud crack, and then a tree right next to them split open, its edges glowing red like embers from a roaring fire.

"Lightning!" Xavier said. But not normal lightning. This lightning was way too close—as if it was aiming straight for *them.* Another crack, and another nearby tree split and shriveled, burned to a crisp in an instant.

"Watch out!" Xavier cried. They dodged out of the way as the blackened tree began to topple over, crashing to the ground in a shower of sparks. Evan felt his courage evaporate. If this was a dream, it was getting way too scary: the deadly lightning, the falling trees, the growing rumble that seemed to shake the forest to its roots, the ominous blackening of the sky. Evan wanted to wake up now.

He felt his brother's hand on his shoulder. "Let's keep going," Xavier said, as if knowing what Evan was thinking. "Just . . . don't look back, whatever you do."

Evan nodded, fighting back tears. He wouldn't let Xavier see *that*, that's for sure. He looked toward the purple leaves, the trail that seemed to be their only way forward. The darkness was closing in around them.

Evan heard the creature's voice in his head. Kind of like his own, but different somehow. Deeper. More certain of itself. *Stay on the trail. Don't look back,* it said.

So Evan didn't.

Xavier could just make out the little creature in the robe, darting this way and that, drenching the leaves of the trees in brilliant purple as it went. How did it move so fast? Xavier couldn't even tell if it had legs.

He kept checking to make sure Evan was still with him—he couldn't lose his brother. Mom would kill him.

Mom. Dad. Where were they? What was this world he and his brother had jumped into? He glanced up at the purple-red sky, which seemed to be moving, swirling almost, like a storm gathering. A bad one. All around him trees were splitting open, glowing red and then shriveling, falling, and sending up billows of ashes. Charred, smoldering branches rained down on either side of them, so close Xavier could feel the hot embers prickling his skin. He swatted at them as if they were alive, like swarming mosquitos. Maybe Evan was right—maybe this really was a dream and nothing bad could happen to them. Maybe. But Xavier had never felt a shivering in his soul like this in any other dream before.

He heard a high-pitched yelp and turned to see Evan trapped beneath a fallen tree branch. Above him, the rest of the seared tree was creaking and popping as it started to tip over. Xavier ran back to Evan, who was clawing the thick muck to free himself.

"I'm stuck!" Evan cried, panicking now as the falling tree loomed over them. Xavier lifted the branch and grabbed hold of his brother, ripping the bottom of Evan's pant leg as he pulled him up. The boys scrambled away just as the tree crashed behind them in a fountain of glowing ash.

"Ouch!" Evan wiped some ash off his arm where it burned his skin a little.

"You okay?" Xavier asked.

"Yeah, I think so."

Xavier tried to look at Evan's arm, but his brother pulled away roughly.

Don't stop! The voice again, in their heads, bouncing off the trees. Xavier and Evan lurched once more toward the purple path. Behind them the falling trees made hideous noises, like agonizing screams. *Do trees feel pain?* Xavier wondered. It sounded to him like the whole world was crying out in terror and fear, the darkness closing in on them.

Where are we going? When are we going to get there? Will this ever end? he wondered.

And then suddenly it did. The trail opened to a large body of water, its still surface reflecting the blotched red and purple sky. The water seemed to have no end—as big as an ocean, stretching to the stormy horizon. It was eerily calm in contrast to the backdrop of crashing trees and crackling lightning, the ever-growing rumble like an earthquake gathering under their feet. The water didn't move, not even a ripple.

"Whoa," said Evan. He was panting, his hands on his knees. He glanced behind him, poised to bolt if necessary. "Where do we go now?"

Xavier had no answer. It seemed as though they were trapped between the black trees and the tranquil water—there was nowhere else *to* go.

"Follow me!"

Both boys jumped, turning their attention to the lake. There, hovering over the mirrorlike surface of the water, was the purple-robed creature. *"Into the Water!"* the voice boomed, nearly drowning out the sounds of chaos behind them. Then the creature just—disappeared, like it was sucked right into the water.

Into the water? Xavier took a breath, wondering what it meant.

"He'll come back, right?" said Evan. He had to shout to make himself heard over the noise of the world collapsing behind them. "He just went to get us—a boat?"

"*Under* the water?" Xavier shouted back. "You think maybe he went to get us a submarine?"

"It's just a dream!" Evan cried, lifting his head with newfound confidence. As if he was trying to convince himself. "It's like *Kingdom Quest*."

"So we're dreaming we're in a video game? Both of us? Together?"

"Sure!" said Evan. "Why not? Anything can happen in a dream. Hey, look!"

Evan pointed at the water. Xavier looked. The still surface had begun to ripple slightly, changing color. An image appeared on the water, golden, as if touched by an unseen sun.

"It's that thing from my book again!" Evan cried, pointing. "Let's go!"

"You're going in?" asked Xavier. He couldn't believe it—was this the same kid who earlier that day had been afraid to jump in the pond? Then he remembered—this was a dream. That's what Evan thought, anyway. Although it seemed less and less like a dream to Xavier.

Another jolt of lightning cracked right over their heads. The rumbling sound had become deafening— Xavier had the impression that some giant boulder was rolling straight toward them, flattening everything in its path.

"Hurry!" Evan cried. He turned and leaped into the water with both feet.

"Evan!" Xavier tried to grab his brother, but he was already gone, the water swallowing him up, closing over him like a door. Xavier was left standing help-lessly at the edge of the lake. He thought he saw a faint tinge of red appear on the glassy surface. He hoped he would wake up soon, before this dream got any worse.

CHAPTER FOUR

Into the Cave

*A*m *I underwater?*
    Evan opened one eye, sure he wouldn't be able to see a thing in the murk below the water. Something about this water didn't feel like water. It wasn't cold—it wasn't even *wet.*

He slowly opened the other eye and gazed around him at a shimmering world of blue and silver, little white bubbles of light floating lazily, flickering slightly, as if catching rays of sunlight from the world above. He raised an arm and found it moved freely, not like it was suspended in water. There *was* no water, he realized. He took a cautious breath. Air filled his lungs. Real air. Oxygen. He wasn't underwater at all. In fact, he was completely *dry.*

He was standing—not floating, not swimming. On a floor. A solid floor. Rock. He looked down at his clothes. His torn and muddy pajamas were gone, replaced by a gray shirt and smooth, leatherlike pants. The symbol from his book about Ahoratos was emblazoned on the shirt in silver. He touched it, and it flickered slightly.

Where am I?

He turned in a slow circle, taking it all in. A cave? He'd visited a cave once. This place sort of looked like that, with all sorts of random rock formations—what were they called? *Stalactites and stalagmites.* The stalactites dripped from the ceiling like giant icicles. But these glowed a silvery blue, like they were lit from within. The stalagmites rose up from the floor like small, glistening mountain ranges. Even the walls had a strange, otherworldly glow. What sort of place had he landed in? An undersea cave with no water? And where was Xavier?

Evan took a step, and then another, hoping to see more of the cave. He noticed several tunnels going off in different directions, but they were completely dark. Was he supposed to go down one of them? He didn't see the little purple guy anywhere.

Suddenly there was a grinding noise, like a garbage disposal trying to chew up something way too big. Evan jumped away, startled, and whipped around to see his brother standing there next to him, completely dry and dressed the same as him. It was as if the garbage disposal had coughed him up, all in one piece. Xavier had a goofy look on his face, like he had no idea what just happened. Made sense. Evan didn't know what was going on either. But he'd gotten there first, so for once he had something to brag about.

"'Bout time you showed up," he said confidently, so Xavier wouldn't know how rattled he was on the inside. And then, under his breath: "Chicken."

Xavier didn't respond to the jibe. He was too busy looking around in slack-jawed wonder at the fantastic glowing formations of this world in which they'd found themselves.

"Is it real?" he asked finally, as if he needed help making up his mind. "Are we underwater?"

"We went into the water, but we're not in it anymore," Evan said thoughtfully. He'd had more time to work this out. "It's like we went right *through* the water and ended up here. Underneath."

"Under the water? All dry? And in different clothes?"

"Yeah, cool," Evan said. "But hey, if it's a dream, anything can happen, right?"

"What are those?" Xavier said, pointing to the flecks of light dancing in random patterns around them, some almost infinitesimal and others as big as dandelion puffs. Evan reached out to grab one, but it darted away.

"Welcome to Ahoratos, young princes."

Both boys jumped. An enormous voice filled the chamber, making the stalactites and stalagmites shiver. The little figure in the purple robe was before them again, appearing from nowhere, radiating light, its face still in shadow.

"You are safe here."

They assumed it was the creature that had spoken, yet the voice seemed to come from everywhere in the room, like many different echoes converging all at once. How could a thing so small have such a big voice? And yet, there was something large about this creature, despite its diminutive size. Something sort of—regal too. Something that made both Xavier and Evan believe what it was saying. *We're safe.*

Evan approached the creature cautiously, hoping to get a better look. It didn't actually move, yet wherever Evan stepped, its face remained hidden.

"Are you a troll?" he asked slowly.

"Evan!" said Xavier, embarrassed. Evan ignored him.

"An elf?"

"I. Am. Ruwach." Each word was like its own sentence, which made it seem all the more important.

"Roo-*who*?" Evan asked, his nose wrinkling.

"Ru-wach," said the purple trollish, elfish creature in a measured tone. "I am your guide in Ahoratos."

"Ru-wok." Evan repeated the name, slowly, as if trying to sort out what it meant. Then he turned to his brother and whispered, "Definitely not a troll."

Xavier spoke up, hoping the elf-troll-whatever-it-was-creature hadn't heard his brother's comment. "Uh, sir? Would you mind just telling us—where we are? And what we're doing here?"

"You are in the Cave," Ruwach said in the same deliberate, booming voice.

Evan chuckled. "Good name for a cave," he said under his breath. Xavier nudged him.

"You must be properly equipped before you can go further. Follow me." Ruwach turned slowly, the glowing emblem of Ahoratos on the back of his robe clearly visible to the boys. Then all at once he took off down one of the dark passageways. As he went, the walls and ceiling lit up with purple lights, similar to the purple leaves in the dark forest, revealing shining objects on either side.

Xavier wasn't sure he wanted to go any further. Evan, however, was starting to relax, as if ready for an adventure. It was, after all, only a dream.

"Armor!" Evan cried, for the objects in the passageway looked very much like armor. "Wow! Sweet!" The sight of the armor made the last of his fear melt away. "Come on, Xavi!"

He dashed off after the smallish, not-a-trollish creature named Ruwach.

"Wait!" Xavier said. "Do you really think it's safe?"

"Hey," Evan replied. "We're in a cave, under a lake, with a little purple dude that's not a troll. What could be safer?"

Xavier hurried to follow his little brother, still not sure if this was the right thing to do, but seeing no other option. The tunnel twisted and turned, sometimes splitting into several more tunnels, sometimes sloping downhill unexpectedly. The strange little creature named Ruwach appeared to be in a big hurry, but the boys didn't have trouble keeping up with him. Xavier felt that he was moving much faster than his legs could actually carry him.

As the passages lit up, the boys saw that there were hundreds, maybe *thousands* of suits of armor displayed on either side of them—breastplates, helmets, belts, boots, shields, swords—all arranged on the walls of the Cave. The armor came in endless varieties and appeared to be from many different times in history. In fact, each set was clearly marked with a date on a small silver placard below it: 1649, 1875, 1947, 2013 . . . And the dates went well into the future. There were pieces made of leather, iron, wood, bronze, and even some odd-colored material Xavier could not identify. Some were very plain, and some had intricate engravings in the breastplates. The helmets were all different shapes and sizes too—Roman, Greek, Viking—and some so fantastic he had never seen them in any history book.

When they were younger, Xavier and Evan and their friends from their old neighborhood used to play Castles and Kings in the basement of their apartment building. The basement was dark and shadowy, with crumbling walls that looked to them like the dank stone walls of a real castle. They staged mock tournaments (using skateboards for horses) and epic battles with swords they'd made out of yardsticks and old pieces of baseboard trim they'd found lying around. They made breastplates out of cardboard and scraps of aluminum foil.

But this armor—*this armor*—looked real. Xavier longed to stop and touch it, just to make sure, but they were moving too fast.

Next to each suit of armor was a heavy door fastened with a large padlock. What was behind those doors? Whoever heard of doors in a cave anyway? Xavier suspected there was something very important and interesting behind them—he longed to know what it was.

He was so busy looking at the armor and the doors that he almost crashed into Ruwach, who had stopped suddenly in the middle of the tunnel. Evan wasn't looking either and slammed into Xavier's back before sprawling on the ground with a yelp. Xavier turned around to help him up.

"Thanks for the warning," Evan muttered.

"Watch where you're going next time."

Then Ruwach slowly stretched out his arms—Xavier hadn't realized he *had* arms. They were far longer than the rest of him, but draped in purple so his hands were not visible. He was pointing toward the armor beside him, which lit up as if in a spotlight. Evan crept closer to get a better look.

"Hey! That's my name!" Evan said in surprise, pointing to a placard where his full name and birth date were written in fancy gold lettering. "And there's yours, Xavi! They have *our* names on them! And our birthdays too! Awesome!"

Xavier looked and saw his own name and birth date in the same gold lettering next to another set of armor. *Wow.* There it was. His very own armor.

But the armor—it didn't look like armor at all! At least not like any kind Xavier had ever seen before. The breastplate was white, made of a smooth plastic-looking material, and vaguely triangular, like some sort of space-age dinner platter. There was a large round orb in the center, kind of purply-gray. A wide belt hung just below the breastplate, plain white without even a buckle.

The boots sat on their own little shelf at the bottom. They were white and of the same material as the breastplate—very smooth and plain. Beside the breastplate and belt was a large golden shield with that weird emblem in the center. A white rounded helmet, not unlike a bike helmet but sleeker, with less padding and a curvy edge, sat just above the breastplate.

Hanging above all the pieces, just out of reach, was a long, elegant sword, the tiny emblem of Ahoratos engraved in the golden hilt.

Both boys stared at their armor, examining every piece. Before either could ask another question, Ruwach spoke.

"When you come to Ahoratos, you must put on your armor as quickly as possible. You cannot be here without it. You can always find it in the Cave, and you must enter the Cave through the Water. It is the only way in. Do you understand?"

The boys stared blankly at Ruwach for a moment or two.

"This doesn't look like real armor," said Evan finally, clearly disappointed. Xavier was thinking the same thing, but he never would have spoken it aloud.

"You will never have victory in Ahoratos unless you are equipped," Ruwach continued, ignoring Evan's comment.

"But this is just a dream, right? Just an imaginary place," Xavier said with a knowing nod, trying to convince himself.

Ruwach tilted his hooded head down and cocked it to the left a little. His right arm rose to chest level and rested where his heart might have been. "Ahoratos is the *real* world," he said. "And here, you are who you're always supposed to be. You are Prince Warriors."

"Prince Warriors?" Evan perked up. "Prince Warriors! Like in my book! Cool!"

"I think you might have the wrong people," said Xavier, shaking his head. "I mean, we're just kids. We aren't princes. And we're *definitely* not warriors."

"Here in Ahoratos, you are," Ruwach said. His voice was softer now, almost whispery, although Xavier could not quite figure out which direction it came from. "The world you live in day to day—that world is but a shadow of the Real World. This is the world where the battles rage, where your real enemy lies."

Evan's ears perked up—he suddenly remembered the talk he'd had with his mom before he went to bed. Battles . . . an enemy . . . an enemy who was *not* Xavier.

"What kind of battle?" Evan asked suddenly.

"You like battles, do you?" Ruwach's voice had changed, become softer and yet more definitive. Evan knew he was talking about the battles between his brother and him, like the fight on the dock. He glanced at Xavier, who was looking at the ground, as if he knew it too.

"You must learn who your real enemy is," Ruwach said, his voice even softer. Evan felt a chill at his tone. *Your real enemy . . .*

"Up there, above the water—the trees and stuff . . ." Evan whispered. "What *was* all that?"

"What did you see?" Ruwach asked.

"It got darker and darker, and the trees were falling, and the whole world was falling apart—"

"Chaos," Xavier said suddenly, remembering the word he'd looked up earlier that evening. *Tumult. Chaos. The Riot Act.*

"Chaos is the work of the enemy," Ruwach responded with a nod of his hood, as if he approved of Xavier's assessment. "The enemy will do everything in his power to distract you, to discourage you, to delay you, to defeat you. He is always near in Ahoratos. This is his dwelling place. The evidence of his schemes is much more apparent in Ahoratos than it is on earth, which is why you must be properly equipped when you are in this realm. The victory you achieve here will determine the outcome of the battles you face there."

"What's behind those doors?" Evan asked. He'd started nosing around. "Is it a dungeon or something? Can we see?"

"In good time."

"What about the sword? Can I try it out? It looks pretty heavy—"

"Belt first." Ruwach gestured toward the belt that hung on the wall. Evan reached out to touch it.

"No—" Ruwach said, but too late. As Evan's fingers grazed the belt, there was a flash of light and he was propelled backward and knocked to the ground. He let out a soft "Ow!" and winced in pain.

"You okay?" Xavier asked, rushing over to help him.

"I'm fine," Evan said, turning away from his brother and shaking out his hand as if he'd been burned. He struggled to his feet. "No big deal."

Xavier backed away, looking at his brother with concern. Although he seemed okay, he'd been knocked back pretty hard. And what was that flash? It must have hurt.

"The armor must be received. I must give it to you, then it is your responsibility to put it on and use it," Ruwach said. He took the belt from the wall and held it up. Strange symbols appeared on its plain surface. As Evan and Xavier stared, the symbols began to pulse and shift, becoming a word:

T-R-U-T-H

"Why does it say *truth*?" Evan asked.

"The belt holds everything together."

Ruwach offered no explanation for this cryptic response. He handed the boys their belts. Xavier took his, not sure what to do with it. There was no way to buckle it on. He waited for instructions, but Ruwach said nothing. He looked at Evan, who held the belt this way and that, trying to figure out how it was supposed to fit. Finally, Xavier gave up and wrapped it around his waist, like he would a belt for a bathrobe. As he did, the belt seemed to take on a life of its own, snaking around his body and conforming to his size. The two ends fused together so perfectly that the edges were invisible.

"Whoa," said Evan. "Sweet." He was eager to try it himself—he wrapped his belt around his waist, and it fitted to him just as Xavier's had. He glanced at Xavier and grinned as if to say: *Dream, right?*

Ruwach then took down Xavier's breastplate and handed it to him. Xavier looked at it doubtfully. It didn't have any straps to buckle. But then, neither did the belt, and that worked. So he placed it against his chest. Instantly he felt it changing, shaping, conforming to his size, just as the belt had. The breastplate stuck to him like it had been sewn on, fitting perfectly. He waited for it to do something, for the orb to light up or flash or display a word. But nothing happened. He was a little disappointed.

"This thing will never stop an arrow or a sword blow," Evan said after putting on his own breastplate. "It's not even metal. It's like plastic or something. Plus, it's too small! Doesn't even cover my whole middle. What's it good for?" He looked at the non-trollish guy, hoping for a real answer this time. But there wasn't one.

Xavier didn't say so, but he sort of agreed. The breastplate seemed more like a nifty fashion accessory—something a futuristic space ninja would wear—than a functional piece of armor.

Maybe it changes when you go into battle, Xavier thought. He hunted around on the breastplate for an On switch. He didn't see one.

"Boots." Ruwach handed both boys their boots, which they hurried to put on. Despite not having any laces or buckles, the boots slid on easily, conforming to the boys' feet just as the belts had done. They were pretty comfortable and even had ventilation slats by the ankles, so it was easier to walk. Evan took a few practice steps, but he wasn't overly impressed.

"Great. Now do we get the swords?"

"Evan," Xavier warned.

"You have everything you need," said Ruwach finally. And that was it.

Ruwach moved toward them. "Remember, these three pieces you must wear at all times when in Ahoratos. Do you understand?"

"Okay, but what about the swords?" Evan asked. He was trying hard not to sound impolite, but it didn't seem right that they should get these three pieces only and not the rest. Did Ruwach expect them to go into battle half-dressed?

"Battles in Ahoratos do not look the same as battles on earth, therefore they cannot be fought the same," Ruwach said, as if he had read Evan's mind. "That is something you will learn, Prince Evan. You too, Prince Xavier."

"But why *us*?" Xavier asked. "Why are *we* here?"

"You were chosen," Ruwach paused, and the cadence of his words changed. Slower. Sadder. "Many are chosen, but few come."

"Maybe they would if the armor looked a little more—*armor-ish*," Evan said sarcastically. He glanced at Xavier, laughing a little, but stopped when he saw the disgusted look on his brother's face. Xavier let out a long breath. He wished Evan wouldn't say *everything* that came to his mind.

"So what do we do now?" Evan continued, in a less sarcastic tone of voice. "Hang around here until this enemy comes along?"

"You will soon see. First, we must go and get the others." Ruwach spun swiftly and began to do that funny walk-run-waddle thing he did down the winding tunnel.

"What others?" cried Evan as the boys took off after Ruwach. "You mean there are *more*?"

CHAPTER FIVE

Water in the Desert

Evan and Xavier sped down more tunnels until they found themselves once again in the room where they'd first entered the Cave. They didn't see any *others* there—nothing moved but the floating balls of light.

Ruwach didn't speak but unfolded his long arms to the ceiling, his hooded head facing up as well. The boys looked up, wondering what Ruwach was looking at (assuming he had actual eyes). They couldn't see anything except rows of glowing blue stalactites. Then Ruwach began rotating his arms in a slow, steady circle. As he did, the stalactites grew faint, transparent, until they disappeared altogether, revealing a hole in the top of the Cave, like a window. The boys stared, wondering what it was they were seeing through this "window." At first it was just colors: white and red. And then the shapes became clearer—the white became blowing, drifting sand. And the red became a vast, unbroken sky.

"Whoa," Evan said under his breath. "Is it like TV? Or is it real?"

"Is that Ahoratos?" asked Xavier. "It looks way different from what we saw."

"Yeah," said Evan. "No trees . . . just sand."

"Hey!" Xavier said suddenly. "I see someone!" He could make out two figures, a boy and a girl, walking through the sand. They looked lost and very tired, trudging listlessly, their heads hanging in exhaustion.

"I know those guys." Evan moved a few steps closer, squinting against the bright whiteness of the sandy world above. "They're kids from the Rec. What are they doing up there?"

"They must find the Water, just as you did," Ruwach said.

"Water?" Evan said. "That place looks like a desert. Where's the Water?"

"The Water is there. It is always there. Call them. Show them the way."

Xavier and Evan looked at each other in confusion. How were they supposed to call to those kids from an underwater cave? They stood there for a moment, doing nothing. Ruwach moved in close to them, so close they could almost feel his whispered words dancing on the back of their necks.

"Call to them. Time is running out."

So, Evan decided to do just that. He wasn't sure what he was supposed to say, but he cupped his hands to his mouth and shouted up to the ceiling.

"Hey! You guys! Over here!"

His voice echoed several times, and to his amazement he could *see* the echoes rippling through the air. They seemed to rise up and hit the invisible barrier separating the Cave from the storm, causing it to tremble.

The ripples caught Xavier's attention as well. "It's like—we *are* under the Water." He scratched his head in disbelief. Evan shouted again, and then Xavier joined him, sending more ripples upward to the opening.

"Over here! In the Water! Find the Water!"

The boy in the desert world suddenly stopped walking and lifted his head, scanning the horizon. He had heard Evan and Xavier's call! Xavier could see who he was now: Levi, Mr. J. Ar's son. Levi hung with the skateboard crowd, the coolest kids at the Rec. Xavier had wanted to bring his skateboard so many times and join them, but he was too intimidated. He couldn't do all the tricks those kids could do. He thought he remembered the girl, too, because she often wore that pink, sparkly hoodie.

Levi walked more purposely, gesturing to the girl to follow him. He was pointing to something. Evan wondered if he could see the Water now.

But then something else drew Xavier's attention away. Above the two kids, the red sky began to change—it was getting darker, streaked with purple and black, just the way it had when he and Evan had been running through the dark, menacing forest. Then he remembered the trees splitting and falling, turning to ashes, like the whole world was burning up. *This can't be good,* he thought.

His eyes fell to the horizon, because he knew what would happen next. His heart started to hammer in his chest. *It* was coming. The enemy. The one Ruwach had told them about. Those two kids needed to find the Water before . . .

Just then a plume of sand rose up from the ground on the horizon. The wind was picking up, causing more sand to tussle about.

"The chaos is coming," Xavier murmured, to no one in particular.

"What?" said Evan.

"*It's* coming—look!" Xavier pointed.

Evan's face went pale, whitewashed by the memory of what he and his brother had gone through to get to the Water.

The column of sand spun high into the red sky, growing larger as it pulled more and more sand into its vortex. But then more columns sprung out of the center column, as if it were growing arms and legs— and a head. Two bright beams of light radiated from the head shape—like eyes, zeroing in on Levi and Brianna.

"It's—a grobel . . ." said Evan in a soft voice. "A *sand* grobel. There was one of those in my book too."

"A grobel? What's that?" asked Xavier.

"It's a creature—a *bad* creature—made out of something not really alive."

"They need to hurry," Xavier said, the fear creeping down the back of his neck. He put his hands to his mouth, filled his lungs with more oxygen than he thought they could hold, and yelled: "Hurry! Get to the Water!"

———

Levi saw it too—the huge mound of sand with burning white eyes, growing legs and arms that got bigger and bigger. This was no ordinary sandstorm.

"Run!" he shouted to Brianna, taking her hand. He had no idea where to go, but he knew nothing good could come of staying where they were. "Come on, Bean!"

The two kids ran, covering their eyes against the hot wind that stung their faces and coated the insides of their mouths. When that first breeze had wafted across their burning cheeks, they'd been grateful. They needed a breath of breeze after walking in this scorching heat for so long. But *this*? This was not what they'd expected at all.

"Where can we go?" Brianna cried.

Levi heard it again—voices, someone calling. Where was it coming from? He looked ahead of him and saw something—an oasis glimmering on the surface of the sand. Was it really water? Or was it only a mirage?

"Water!" he cried. "We need to get to that water!"

"Water? Where?"

"Hurry . . . Get to the Water . . ."

Was the water talking?

Brianna fell to her knees, unable to move against the wind any longer. "You go look!" she cried. "I'll wait here!" She cowered under her hoodie, trying to protect her face.

"No, you have to come too!" Levi shouted.

"I can't! I can't even see!"

Levi saw it was useless to try and persuade her, so he left her where she was and struggled on, using his weight to push against the full force of the wind. Thankfully, the oasis he had seen did not disappear—although it wasn't exactly what he thought it would be. As he approached, he realized he was seeing not one body of water but several small puddles, as if the oasis had dried up and this was all that was left.

Levi put one hand over his mouth to keep from swallowing the hot air, now mixed with grains of sand that burrowed into his skin. He knelt down before one of the puddles and put his free hand into the water. It was cool and wet, but very shallow, too shallow even to lie in for some protection. He crawled over and tried another, hoping it might be a little deeper. But it wasn't.

He looked over his shoulder at the sand grobel careening toward them, its arms spread wide enough to snatch up anything in its path. The sky—what he could see of it—was a churning canvas of angry colors—red, black, purple. Time was running out. He had to figure out a way to escape, if not for himself, then for Bean. The puddles, meager as they were, were their only hope.

Levi crawled to another puddle, head ducked low against the strengthening wind, and dug his fingers into the wet, muddied sand. It was the same as the one before. He splashed some of the water over his face, wondering how he might be able to bring some over to Bean. Even if he could cup some water in his hands, by the time he got to her it would be dried up or blown away.

He stared at the water. Why was he expecting something to happen? Why had the voices told him to get *into* the water? It was just a puddle.

Get back to Bean. The thought nagged at him. She was still alone. If they were going to be trapped by a monster, they might as well be trapped together. Perhaps he could still protect her somehow. He tried to turn and look for her, but the wind was now so fierce he couldn't see more than a foot in front of him. His eyes were tearing up, but when he reached up to wipe them . . .

He saw a movement, out of the corner of his eye. One of the other puddles rippled as if a rock had been skipped across its surface. The wind, he thought—it would soon blow the water away. Then he heard the voices again, barely audible over the shrieking wind: *"Hurry! Get to the Water!"* The voices seemed to be synced with the ripples. He scrambled over to that puddle and peered in. Once the ripples subsided, he thought he saw his own windblown face mirrored in the water, as he had in all the others. Then he realized it wasn't his face at all. It was something else—it was the thing he had first seen over Landon's head. That strange emblem of Ahoratos!

He called to Brianna, "Bean! Come on! I found it!" His voice was drowned out by the high-pitched whistle of the wind, the eerie sound of millions of grains of sand crashing into each other. "Bean!" he screamed as loud as he could. But she didn't hear him.

"Hurry! Get in the Water!"

Get in the water? What good would that do? It was only a puddle, after all. But the image was there, and the voices still called to him, making the water tremble even more. He touched the water, feeling a pulling sensation, the same thing that had happened when he'd grabbed the weird object hanging over Landon's head.

"Bean! Over here! Get in the water!" It was already pulling him down, his arm, his shoulder, his whole body. He tried one more time yelling out to Brianna. "Over he—"

The Water swallowed him.

CHAPTER SIX

Puddle Jumping

L evi's feet were cold. That seemed strange, since he was completely submerged in water. Wasn't he? He opened his eyes slightly, expecting to see a murky underwater scene. No water. Everything around him glowed blue and white. He let the breath he'd been holding out of his aching lungs. Then he breathed in. He could breathe. Actual air.

He looked down at the floor—stone. No wonder it was cold. He'd been so hot a moment ago, the wind and sand burning his face.

Sand. He reached up and felt his skin. It was smooth. No sand coating. He shook his head and dusted his hands over his curly hair, expecting a shower of sand over his face. But there was nothing. He was dry—and *clean.*

His clothes were different too. Instead of his Tony Hawk T-shirt and jeans, he was wearing thick gray pants and a shirt with that same weird emblem on it— glowing faintly.

He gazed around him at the strange rock forma- tions, the tiny specks of light flitting around his head. He remembered being sucked down into the puddle, the puddle with the symbol. He thought it had just happened a minute ago—but had time passed that he didn't know about? It seemed as though he'd woken up in some other, even weirder, world.

He looked up. Three people stood before him. Two of them were kids, a big one and a smaller one. Was that— Xavier? The basketball kid from the Rec? And his little brother? The other person was—not quite a *person* at all. Like a little purple blob of something with no face.

"Welcome to Ahoratos, Prince Levi," said the purple blob. His voice boomed through the space, and Levi felt it in the pit of his stomach. *So, it must be some sort of person.* As his eyes adjusted, Levi realized that the blob part was actually a robe. "We've been expecting you."

"You have?" Levi's throat felt scratchy. *He knows my name? That's weird. And he called me a prince. That's even weirder.* "Where am I?"

"In the Cave," the younger kid said. He sounded very confident, like he knew what he was talking about. "And that's Reebok. Don't worry. He's not a troll."

"*Ruwach*," said Xavier in a disgusted voice. "Roo-*wok*."

"Right. Roo-*wok*," said the younger kid, pronouncing each syllable like it was a separate word. "And I'm Evan, EH-van, and this is Xavier, ZAV-ee-er, my brother. You're Levi, right? The skateboarder? From the Rec?"

Levi nodded, then shook his head like he was trying to shake the sand out of his brain. "The storm—the water—went in a puddle—saw that weird thing . . ."

"The Crest of Ahoratos," said the purple dude named Ruwach. "That is what led you here."

"So that's what it is!" said Evan. "A crest—like knights had on their shields in the old days. The Crest of A-Horses."

"Ahoratos," Xavier said.

"That's what I said!"

Xavier shook his head and took a step toward Levi. "Your friend is still out there." He pointed up to the ceiling. Levi gazed up in amazement; he could see the monster—the sand grobel—rampaging across the desert through a hole in the ceiling. In the *ceiling*? How was that possible?

"Be—Brianna?" he said. "Where is she?"

Ruwach reached up his really long arms toward the ceiling and began to turn them slowly, and as he did the whole scene shifted perspective to a small mound of pinkish white, nearly lost in the blowing sand. Then Ruwach drew his arms downward, and the scene zoomed in to a close-up. Levi could see now that the mound was Brianna. She wasn't moving at all, like she'd given up the fight.

Levi gasped. "I tried to tell her—she wouldn't come." He thought he might cry and turned his head so the two boys wouldn't see. "I lost her."

"She is not lost." Ruwach stepped toward Levi, but his hooded face was still directed upward, toward Brianna. "Do not fear. I can bring the Water to her."

Ruwach pointed upward, and the view changed again, zooming in on the puddle with the Crest of Ahoratos. Levi watched, doubtful. But then Ruwach waved his arms and—*moved the Water*. Levi blinked in awe as the puddle of water—the Water—zoomed across the stretch of sand until it was right in front of Brianna. She didn't see it, though. Her eyes were shut tight, her face hidden under her arms.

"Call to her," Ruwach said.

"What do you mean?" Levi asked, confused.

"She'll hear you!" Evan said. "You've got to shout real loud."

Levi's brow furrowed. He hesitated.

"Do it!" shouted Evan.

"Uh, okay . . . Bean!" Levi said, not exactly shouting. He felt a little foolish.

"Bean?" Evan said, giggling.

"I mean, Brianna!" Levi said louder, his voice echoing through the Cave. "Brianna! Can you hear me?"

To Levi's amazement, he saw the window above him start to ripple, as if his words had actually struck some invisible barrier.

"That's it," said Evan, encouraging. "Keep going. Tell her to get in the Water!"

"Bean! In the Water! Get in the Water!"

The words rippled the barrier again. Brianna raised her head and opened her eyes slightly, then slammed them shut against the onslaught of sand. Even her eyelashes were coated. Then she opened them again, just enough to look down. When she saw the Water, her eyes widened ever so slightly. She knew that puddle hadn't been there a moment ago.

"Brianna! Bean! Get in the Water! It's right there!" Levi's voice was getting stronger, louder. She could hear him!

Brianna put one hand out cautiously, touching the surface of the Water very lightly. The barrier rippled again.

"She sees it!" Levi said. Ruwach *had* brought the Water right to her. "Get in, Bean! Get in the Water!" he shouted over and over. The other boys joined in.

Brianna still seemed hesitant. The wind picked up, the storm so dense now it was difficult to see her at all, other than a few glittery specks of her headband.

"Don't give up, Bean!" Levi looked around frantically and saw a series of ledges in the rock formations of the Cave. He ran to them, leaping from one to the other so he could get close enough to the ceiling. Then he tried to plunge his hand through the barrier, in hopes of reaching her. But the invisible barrier just snapped back like a trampoline, knocking him off his feet. He tumbled down the rocks, groaning.

"She must come through on her own," said Ruwach calmly. "Others can call her, and I can make it accessible for her, but she must make the choice on her own."

The other two boys shouted and threw small pebbles up to the ceiling, making more ripples. Levi scrambled back up on the ledge, joining their chorus, punching the barrier with his hands.

"Bean! Get in!" He didn't care anymore that the others heard him call her Bean. All that mattered was getting her out of the storm and into the Water.

Brianna squinted at the puddle of water in front of her, the symbol of Ahoratos—the one they'd seen over Landon's head—shining on the surface. The voices sounded again, as if coming from the puddle itself: *Get in!*

She felt sand in her ears, in her mouth, in her nostrils even. The sand grobel loomed over her, its huge sand arms wrapping around her, making it harder and harder to breathe.

Yet the water kept talking to her.

She touched it and felt a pulling, a tugging. She pulled away, the sensation too strange. But the water felt cool, such a relief from the hot, stinging sand. She dipped her whole hand in again. The water began tugging on her hand, pulling her down. She tried to resist, but it felt so nice, so cool and wet and un-sandy. She let it pull her, her arm, her shoulder. She shut her eyes as it pulled her down, into the darkness.

Brianna coughed, nearly choking on the suffocating sand. She danced around and waved her arms in the air, as if still fighting off the grobel. She shook her head frantically to get the sand out of her hair, her face, her mouth, but it took her a moment to realize there was no storm anymore. Her skin felt cool but not wet.

She finally opened her eyes, surprised that she could without getting pummeled with sand. She stood very still, taking in her surroundings. Only her eyes roved about—up, down, left, right. Her pink hoodie and striped pants were gone. She was wearing a long gray shirt and leggings. And, strangest of all, there was no sand on her, or water either for that matter. Maybe she had dreamed that she was being chased by a monster made of sand. Maybe she was still dreaming—a dream within a dream.

She felt something grasp her shoulder, and she jumped, giving out a little pant of fright.

"Bean! Are you all right?"

She spun around, her mouth dropping open in amazement. "Levi?" She stared at him, shocked that he was there too.

"I was calling you and calling you. I was scared— you looked like you weren't . . ." He didn't finish. She noticed he was all dry and sand-free as well, and wearing clothes almost identical to hers, with the symbol for Ahoratos glowing on his chest. This was getting *so* weird.

"Where are we?"

"In a cave, I think."

"A cave?"

"*The* Cave," said a voice. She turned to see who had spoken. She saw two boys and—a purple bunny?—standing together a few feet away, staring at her. The boys had on the same clothes as she and Levi, except they were also wearing some strange accessories—white plates on their chests, belts, and sleek white boots. Like they were about to play a game of laser tag.

"What—?" she blurted. "How come I'm not all sandy?" She touched her hair—it wasn't sandy or even messy. Her headband was still in place.

"There is no sand on you, Princess," said another voice, a very deep, resonant voice that echoed all around her. "The Water has made you clean."

She stared at the purple creature—did it just talk? And did it call her a . . . *princess*?

"What's going on?" She turned back to Levi. "We were being attacked by a sand monster thing, and then we went into a puddle? And ended up—here?"

"That's one of the rules," said the little kid, striding forward. "You always have to come through the Water to get to the Cave. That's really important. Don't forget it. And then you have to get your armor on. Right, Mr. . . . Redneck?"

The older kid sighed, like he was annoyed. "Sorry about him. I'm Xavier, and this is my brother Evan. We just got here too."

"Here where?" Brianna asked.

"Welcome to Ahoratos," said the talking purple bunny. No, it wasn't a bunny, but it didn't appear to have a face. Maybe it was a fairy. "I am Ruwach, your guide while you are here."

"He's not a troll," said Evan.

"Evan!" said Xavier.

"Ahoratos," Brianna repeated, not quite believing it.

"Apparently you were right about how to pronounce it," Levi said.

"We're actually there?" Brianna asked. "In Ahoratos? Like from my book?" She blinked a few times, as if still trying to get sand out of her eyes. "Were you guys being chased by a sand monster too?"

"It was a sand *grobel*," corrected Evan, full of confidence. "And no, we were in a forest where all the trees were falling on us. And then we came to a big lake, and we saw that symbol—the Crest—and we got in. That's what you have to do when you see the Crest on the Water—you gotta get in fast. Good thing you did."

"Yeah," Brianna said, still sounding a bit confused. "I guess so."

Levi put his hand on her shoulder. "Hey, Bean," he said softly. "It's okay. We're okay. Right?"

"Stellar," she said weakly, managing a smile. "I'm just a little—you know—wigged out right now. I mean, that monster, grobel thing . . . and this cave . . . How did we get into that desert in the first place?"

"You were in a time of trouble." Ruwach spoke gently now, as if he knew what they'd gone through.

"Yes," said Levi. "There was this bully that was making trouble, and that weird symbol—the Crest—was hanging over his head. It looked so real, so we grabbed it, and the next thing we knew—we were in that desert! And then that monster . . ."

"Grobel," said Evan.

"Yeah, whatever. It started coming for us and—"

"The enemy knows when you enter Ahoratos, so you must always get to the Water immediately—you must come through the Water to enter the Cave," said Ruwach. "It is dangerous to be in Ahoratos—unequipped."

"Like I told you," said Evan. "They need to get their armor. Right, Ru?"

"Don't call him that," Xavier said, flicking Evan lightly on the back of the head with his finger.

"Quit it!" Evan said, waving him away.

Ruwach nodded his hooded head. "Yes. Your armor. You two must follow me." He turned toward Xavier and Evan and gave a simple slow nod as if to say: *Stay out of trouble until we get back.* Then Ruwach took off down one of the dark tunnels, which lit up purple as he went.

"Better follow him," Evan said. "He doesn't wait."

"Come on, Bean," said Levi, still confused but grabbing Brianna by the hand. "Let's go!"

"Armor?" Brianna turned her nose up at the sight of Xavier's and Evan's attire. "There's no way I'm wearing that!"

She continued to protest as Levi dragged her toward the dark path.

CHAPTER SEVEN

The Book

When Levi and Brianna returned to the main room of the Cave, Evan and Xavier stared at them openmouthed.

"What's with that?" Evan said, pointing to Brianna's armor, which was similar to the boys' but embedded with tiny sparkles so it glistened in the dim light of the Cave. Even her belt and boots seemed iridescent, like they'd been dipped in her signature lip gloss. "Armor isn't supposed to sparkle!"

"It's *my* armor," said Brianna, putting her hands on her hips. "It can be sparkly if it wants to." She was clearly delighted with her new accessories. "Just wish I had my lip gloss," she added under her breath.

Levi's armor looked pretty much like the other boys'. The trip through the tunnels had been—a *trip*. He wished he'd had his skateboard with him. Ruwach didn't talk much, nor did he explain what the doors with the padlocks were for. Levi really wanted to know what was in those rooms. Brianna had been too pre-occupied with her shiny armor to pay much attention.

"It looks funny," muttered Evan.

"You look funny too," Brianna sniffed. "Whoever saw a six-year-old wearing armor?"

"I'm almost ten!" Evan shouted.

"What*ever*!" Brianna said, flipping her hair imperiously.

"Young Warriors . . ." Ruwach's thundering voice stopped their bickering. They turned to look at him, sensing a warning in the stillness of his hooded figure. Ruwach lifted one arm and pointed to something hovering in the air that hadn't been there a moment ago. It was a large scroll. He made a movement with his arm, and it rolled open, revealing a list of statements written one after the other in a fancy script.

"There are some things you must remember in order to secure victory in Ahoratos." He spoke each one aloud while the children read along on the scroll:

#1 Always enter the Cave through the Water.

#2 Always put on your armor immediately.

#3 Never leave anything in Ahoratos.

#4 Never take anything back to your world with you.

"So we can't take this armor back with us?" Evan asked with a crestfallen look. He really wanted to show the armor off to his friends. Although it wasn't exactly fearsome, it did have some cool features.

Ruwach's hood swiveled in Evan's direction. "Not right now—but in time. Be patient, young prince."

"Fine," Evan said with a sigh. "Can we get going now?"

Ruwach didn't answer. Instead he turned away from them and faced one of the long, dark corridors. Far in the distance, the kids could see a small speck of something golden hovering in midair. It was too far away to tell exactly what it was. Ruwach stretched both of his long arms toward the tunnel once again, and when he did a strong beam of light burst straight out of the ceiling over the object, illuminating it. It stood out against the backdrop of the darkened, dreamy cave walls. Ruwach drew in his arms, as if he was pulling the object toward them. As he did, it began moving toward them at an impossible speed.

"Watch out! It's gonna crash!" said Evan, diving behind a stalagmite for safety. Levi instinctively grabbed hold of Brianna's arm and pulled her back from the oncoming object—she, naturally, had been moving toward it, wanting to get a better view.

Oddly, it stopped suddenly in the center of the Cave, still bathed in the golden light, hovering just above the floor. The light above dimmed so the kids could actually see what it was. Their eyes widened.

A book.

A *big* book, sitting on a golden pedestal.

It didn't look like any book the kids had ever seen before. It *was* a book, they knew that, but it was luminous and pulsing faintly, as if it was not quite there at all. The golden cover was very plain, with no title or image except the Crest of Ahoratos. But the Crest itself was not stagnant; it rotated slowly, projecting out of the book like a 3-D image. The kids stared in awe.

"This is The Book," said Ruwach. "It was written by the Source. It provides you with your instruction, which will help you stand against the enemy."

"Who's the Source?" asked Xavier.

"The Source of all things: all life, all truth, all wisdom. The Book contains all you ever need to have victory in Ahoratos and on earth."

Ruwach reached one arm toward The Book. The children half expected it to move at lightning speed as it had before. Instead, the cover flipped open, just like a normal book. Except it made a noise—like a musical note—as it lay back against the pedestal. A little spray of light lifted from the first page, as if the sound itself were visible. Ruwach made another quick move with his arm, and the pages of the book began to turn, fanning open, each page playing its own soft note. The notes harmonized into something like a song, filling the Cave with a strange, vibrant music.

Ruwach raised a hand, and the pages stopped flipping, the music still trembling in the air faintly. The kids leaned in to get a closer look. The page Ruwach had stopped on was filled with letters and words that didn't make sense. Like a code, mysteriously scrambled.

"Is that some new language?" Brianna asked.

"This Book is different from any other. It cannot simply be read. It must be revealed. You may not understand the revelation at first, but if you keep it close, you will soon see its meaning. Each instruction you receive from The Book will be stored here." He pointed to the orb on Brianna's breastplate. The children all looked at their own breastplates and then back at Ruwach. Now they were really confused.

"Prince Xavier, step forward."

Xavier took a tentative step toward the shining book. And, without being told, he knelt. He wasn't sure why; he just thought he should. There was something about this moment that felt sacred.

Ruwach nodded his hooded head and touched the page of The Book. The cryptic message began to glow and shift, coming to life. Then the letters themselves lifted off the page and floated into the air above them:

Aort hth Armu oal etF Whhn

ytelrfd eaew oolwl dgt wply ioo Ithi

Before their eyes, the letters slowly began to move, dancing around and rearranging until they formed a whole phrase:

Follow the Way of the Armor.
It will lead you down the right path.

Xavier read the words over and over, wondering what they meant. The Way of the Armor? Then Ruwach reached up and grabbed one of the letters—plucked it right out of the air. When he did, the rest of them trailed behind, as if they were all connected. He gathered them together in his arms and tossed them toward Xavier. Xavier was too shocked to move as he watched each letter flow into the orb of his breastplate, accompanied by the same soft music that had filled the Cave when the pages of The Book had turned. The orb started to glow very faintly, an iridescent purple, like the golden words were spinning right under the surface. Xavier took a breath, as if breathing the words themselves into his lungs, feeling them take root, embedding into his very soul. It was strange and astounding—the most refreshing breath he'd ever taken.

"Whoa," he said softly. He glanced up at Evan, whose mouth dropped open, although no words came out this time. Evan was completely speechless, like he was when he first saw Ruwach in his bedroom.

"Prince Evan," Ruwach said. Evan jumped, then moved slowly next to Xavier. He knelt as well, now in total reverence of this strange, wonderful Book.

Ruwach turned the pages of The Book just as he had before. When the pages slowed, Evan's heart began to race in anticipation of what his instructions might be. The pages stopped turning, and Ruwach pointed to words he'd been planning for Evan since before time began— they too lifted off the page and hovered in the air:

leoFh oelcnte pupw yanta ddso filo lfd ha lwio

Once again, the letters transformed to spell the true instruction.

> *Follow the paths of old, and you will find peace.*

"What's that mean?" Evan asked, his eyebrows furrowing. "The paths of old?" But Ruwach didn't answer him. Instead, he grasped the words and flung them into Evan's orb, so it glowed, humming softly. Evan took in a deeper breath than he'd ever remembered. He glanced at Xavier, who put his hand on Evan's shoulder, smiling faintly.

"Prince Levi," Ruwach said. He beckoned to Levi, who sauntered over to where the other two boys were kneeling. But he didn't kneel. He shifted onto one leg uncomfortably.

Ruwach didn't seem to notice. He just made the pages turn again. They flipped rapidly until a new page appeared, the scrambled-up words straightening out and floating in the air.

> *The gate to destruction is wide,*
> *and the road that leads there is easy to follow.*

Levi's eyebrows scrunched together—he looked confused. The message sounded more like a warning than friendly advice. Not like Evan's and Xavier's. He watched as Ruwach transferred the words to his own orb, seeing the glow like the others, hearing the music. And he was surprised by the full breath he *had* to take when the words came to him.

Brianna stepped up next to him. She looked at the two kneeling boys and at Levi, then shrugged and waited for Ruwach to show her her instruction.

Ruwach, without a word, flipped to a new page in The Book and revealed it to her:

My truth shall lead you to
my house on the holy hill.

Brianna smiled in satisfaction.

"There is one more instruction you all must have," Ruwach said, once he had given the words to Brianna's orb. He touched another page, and the words appeared before them:

Guard your heart above all else,
for it determines your path.

Ruwach did that grabbing thing again, and the words went into all four of their breastplates with a final musical chord. The orbs glowed a little brighter.

"Now," Ruwach said, "you will see your destination as soon as you leave the Cave. But be sure to follow the armor. It will guide you."

"What is the destination?" Brianna asked. "Is it a house, like my instruction said? Like a castle maybe? With unicorns?"

"When you see it, you will know."

"That's it?" Xavier frowned a little. It didn't seem like nearly enough information. "No map? Or even a description of where we're headed? I mean, if we're supposed to be fighting a battle—"

Ruwach's voice stopped Xavier cold—it boomed off the walls of the Cave, making the stalactites tremble, echoing into each kid's heart:

"You have everything you need."

The walls of the Cave quivered, like when the picture on a TV starts cutting out. The kids looked around, startled. When they turned back, Ruwach had disappeared.

Then the Cave itself disappeared, like the TV had been shut off.

It was just—*gone*.

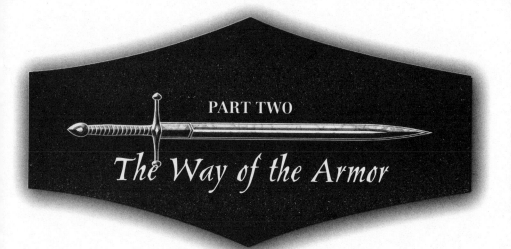

PART TWO

The Way of the Armor

CHAPTER EIGHT

The Gate to Destruction

The kids found themselves in the middle of the sandstorm that they thought they'd left behind for good. They stood with their backs together, their bodies tense. The sand cloud was so thick and the wind so fierce they couldn't see any light coming through, no hint of sky or sun.

"Is it the grobel thing again?" Brianna asked, covering her head in defense against the giant, horrible sand monster that had almost buried her before.

"Hey," Levi said, looking at his hands in wonder. "There's no wind."

He was right. Although the storm raged all around them, they couldn't feel any sand whipping their faces. It was like they were in a protective bubble—or an invisible force field.

"It's like we're in it, but we're not really *in it*," Evan said, his voice hushed. He went up to the edge of the bubble and poked his finger into the barrier. It didn't tremble the way the ceiling of the Cave had. It was solid, hard, and clear like glass. *Clearer* than glass, actually.

"Cool," whispered Xavier to himself.

"So how are we supposed to get out of here?" Brianna asked. "Find this kingdom or whatever?"

As if in answer to her question, loud popping noises sounded all around them, each one announcing trouble. Cracks began to form in the bubble, small at first, but snaking outward like an intricately woven spiderweb.

"This doesn't look good," said Evan.

The kids huddled closer together, as if preparing themselves for the inevitable—the bubble imploding, the storm filling all the space around them. The cracks continued to widen, the creaking noises more pronounced.

"It's opening!" said Brianna, backing away.

"Yeah, but no sand is coming in," Xavier said. He strained forward for a better view. The others followed his lead. It was true: the storm did not enter through the cracks. "They're more like—doorways."

He was right—the cracks had become openings wide enough to see through. Three gates appeared, a big one in the middle and two smaller ones on either side. The middle gate was ornate gold, and the two on the outside were plain, rough wood. Over all three were engraved the words:

Lean not on your own understanding.

Around each doorway, suspended in space, the sandstorm continued to blow. Yet the three doorways opened to three different worlds. The doorway to the left led to a dark, gloomy-looking street with old, crumbling buildings on either side. Two street lamps in the foreground were lit, but the rest weren't. The pavement looked damp, like it was raining.

The gate on the right was the only one that led right back into the raging sandstorm.

The wide middle gate led to a pretty cobbled road, lined with trees and flowers, which stretched over several hills. There were gardens and waterfalls and green mountains, and far into the distance, sitting on a cushion of clouds between the mountain peaks, was a magnificent, sprawling castle.

The sky was clear blue but dotted with odd-shaped objects where clouds should have been, although these things didn't look anything like clouds. They were more like big, floating, grayish-purple rocks.

"The house on the hill!" Brianna said, pointing. "Well, it's more like a house on a cloud than a hill—and that house is more like . . . a castle! Isn't it beautiful?

And that was in my instruction. I'm supposed to go that way!" She lurched toward the middle gate.

"Wait!" Xavier said, reaching out to block her path. "We're supposed to follow the armor, remember? 'Follow the Way of the Armor' . . . whatever that means."

"How do we do that?" asked Levi. "Is it going to talk or something?"

The kids looked at their breastplates, as if waiting for them to speak.

"So what's it saying?" Evan asked. "Can you hear anything?"

Levi and Xavier shook their heads.

"Well, I know I don't want to go that way," Brianna said, pointing to the darkened street to the left. "Looks kind of—*haunted*. And I'm definitely not going back into that sand again. So, there's only one choice." She inched toward the middle gate.

"I agree with her," Evan said. "I mean, why would Ruwach give us this armor and then send us right back into a storm that these two barely made it out of?" He gestured toward Brianna and Levi.

"So what are we waiting for?" asked Levi. "Let's go!"

Suddenly the orb on Levi's breastplate started spinning, the words inside tumbling out so he could see them hovering in the air before him:

The gate to destruction is wide,
and the road that leads there is easy to follow.

The kids read the instruction slowly, carefully, each of their eyes darting from the message to the options before them.

Xavier pointed to the middle gate. "That looks pretty wide. I don't think we're supposed to go that way."

"It doesn't make sense to choose either of those ways," Levi said. "Just look at them!"

Xavier looked—Levi was right. Both options looked pretty uninviting. He took a deep breath.

"Lean not on your own understanding," he said. "It's written right above there, see?"

"That's true," Brianna said thoughtfully. Just then the orb on her breastplate began to spin, glowing faintly.

"Hey, look," said Evan. "Your armor is doing something."

She looked down, straining to see. Then she looked back at Evan. "Yours is doing it too."

They stared in astonishment as both orbs projected a beam of light into the space between them. Particles of light began to dance, twirling around each other until they reorganized into an image: the image of the dark city street that lay through the gate to the left. Then suddenly the image broke apart, the light retreating back into the orbs.

"Whoa," Evan said softly. "I think it wants us to go that way." He pointed to the left gate.

"That way?" Brianna asked, making a face of horror. "That can't be right." She rapped on her breastplate a few times, hoping a new picture would appear. But it didn't.

"I wonder if we're *all* supposed to go that way," Xavier said. "We probably should stay together—" Just then Xavier's orb did the same thing, projecting an image into the air in front of him: the gate with the storm. He looked back up at the gate on the right. "It's telling me to go that way." His shoulders slumped in dismay. "You too." He pointed to Levi. Indeed, Levi's armor was projecting the same image.

"What? No way!" Levi shook his head. "Nuh-uh! Not me. I'm not going back in there."

"But we have armor now," said Xavier.

"This armor? You think this is going to protect us from *that*?" He looked around at the others, who only shrugged, betraying their own doubts about the armor. Levi shook his head. "No way. I'm going this way. Catch you on the flip side." He turned and headed for the middle gate.

Brianna grabbed his arm. "Levi, I don't think you should—"

"Don't worry about me. I'll be in that fancy castle, probably eating an ice cream sundae by the time you guys get there. Have fun!" He approached the gate carefully, took a deep breath, and glanced back at his friends one more time. Then he turned, straightened his shoulders, and stepped over the threshold to the other side. It looked to the other kids as if he had passed through an invisible curtain, the scene of the cobbled road swallowing him as he vanished through it.

Evan rushed over to the middle gate, gazing at the empty scene in awe. "He just—disappeared!"

"I hope he's going to be okay," Brianna said, clearly worried.

"Maybe Levi's right," Xavier said. "Maybe we should just go with him. It does seem like the right way. And maybe we don't know what these pictures really mean . . ." He stopped, his eyes suddenly drawn to the words over the storm gate:

Lean not on your own understanding.

Well, it didn't really make sense, but this was what the armor was telling him to do. He sighed. "I guess I have to go that way." As soon as he said it aloud, he felt something open in himself, a new certainty arising: *Yes, this is the right path.*

"Then I guess we have to go through there," said Brianna, indicating the gateway to the old city street. "It's so dark. And wet. And . . . *old* . . ."

"The old path!" Evan said suddenly, like a light-bulb had come on in his head. "Maybe that's what the instruction meant! Follow the old path!"

"Paths of old, not old path," corrected Brianna.

"Same thing!" Evan said. "It said if I go down the old path, it'll be peaceful or something, right?"

"It said you would *find* peace," said Brianna.

"Well, close enough." Evan marched toward the gate, then stopped and turned. The bright look of confidence on his face had faded already. "So—you coming or what?" he said to Brianna.

"Yeah, I guess so." Brianna sighed deeply, throwing back her shoulders, preparing herself for the worst.

"Hey," said Xavier. Brianna turned to look at him. He was startled by the bigness of her eyes—they were dark brown but sort of sparkly, like the rest of her. He felt his face flush and hoped she didn't notice. "Just watch out for my little brother, okay?"

"I can watch out for myself!" Evan said. With that, he spun around and plunged through the gate. It appeared that he, like Levi, had passed through a curtain and was gone.

"Don't worry," said Brianna, smiling at Xavier. "I got this." She gave him a thumbs-up then turned, took another deep breath, and strode resolutely through the gate after Evan. She disappeared too.

All alone now, Xavier looked down once more at the picture floating on his breastplate. Just to be sure. It hadn't changed. *The storm.* He looked again at the serene middle path that led straight to the castle on the cloud.

"Maybe I'm crazy," he said with a sigh. He walked up to the gate on the right, gazing out at the violent wind, the swirling sand so dense it looked like a thick, dark fog. He straightened, took three huge breaths, shut his eyes, then plunged through the gate and into the storm.

CHAPTER NINE

Walking on Circles

L evi ambled along the cobblestone path, enjoying the warm sunshine, the gentle breeze. It was pretty sweet in Ahoratos, he thought. The sun shone; it was not too hot, not too cold. Around him butterflies fluttered. At least that's what he thought they were, although they didn't really look like any butterflies he'd ever seen before. They were as big as birds, their huge lustrous wings changing color as they flew. They landed on the trees and flowers that lined the road all around him, beating their wings slowly. As he moved along the path they moved too, following his progress, hopping over each other and landing on flowers and tree branches on either side of him. He had a strange feeling they were watching him. After a while he became unnerved by their constant vigilance. He rushed over to a group of them and waved his arms as if to scare them off. They fluttered a bit, but as soon as he returned to his walking, they returned to their watching.

He tried to forget about the butterflies, concentrating on the castle that lay ahead. It looked more fantastical than Disney World. *Maybe there are rides,* he thought. *And food.* He was feeling a bit hungry. Ice cream would be good. Cookies 'n cream. Slathered with hot fudge and whipped cream on top. That would hit the spot.

The castle began to appear as though it was made of frosting and candy—he shook his head, sure his eyes were playing tricks on him. It *was* pretty, though, shimmering on its foundation of clouds, nestled between the tall, hazy, green mountain peaks. He couldn't help but think of Brianna, wishing she had come with him. If she had, she'd likely be making friends with the butterflies and dreaming up a wild story about what was going on in the castle, a story which might include fairies playing dodgeball with gumdrops or racing each other on rainbow-colored unicorns.

The butterflies kept watching him.

Sweat dripped from his brow. He was getting tired from walking so far. How far had he walked anyway? He had no idea.

Wish I had my skateboard.

His boots felt heavy and hot. Despite their ventilation strips, there didn't seem to be any air flowing through them at all. He sat down on a tree stump by the side of the road to take them off. He threw them aside and stretched out his legs, wiggling his toes. *Much better.*

He stood up—the cobbled path felt cool and uncharacteristically smooth under his bare feet, not rough and bumpy like he expected. That was strange. It was, after all, a stone path. But maybe everything in Ahoratos was kind of perfect—even the cobblestones didn't hurt your feet. Awesome.

He glanced down at the tree stump he'd just been sitting on. Something nagged at him, a certain unnamed doubt, settling on his shoulders. He looked around at the path, the sky, the trees, the butterflies—and then back at the tree stump. Hadn't he seen that tree stump before? He remembered, because it had looked like a bear cub from far away.

He walked on for a while in his bare feet, carrying the boots, one in each hand. Another tree stump came into view. He stared at it. Bear cub—*exactly* the same as the last one. And the flowers surrounding it— hadn't he seen those same flowers around the last tree stump too?

The nagging doubt grew even heavier. His eyes darted about, searching for some clue—that was when he realized that all the *trees* were exactly the same as well. Maybe they'd been planted that way, he thought. In a design.

But that tree stump . . .

He was imagining things. It *couldn't* be the same. He looked up at the distant castle on the clouds. *Weird,* he thought. He didn't seem to be getting any closer. He'd been walking for hours already—at least it *felt* like hours—although he couldn't really tell, because the sun hadn't moved in the sky. Maybe it was only minutes. But he was so tired. And the kingdom was still just as far away as it had been when he'd started out.

Something moved behind him. A person? An animal? He whirled to look, but it was gone.

He put down the boots and then reached out to touch the tree stump. It felt smooth and hard, no rough edges, no animal teeth marks, no scent of sap or pine like the stumps in his backyard at home. In fact, this stump looked a lot like the artificial apples his mother kept in a basket on their kitchen table for decoration. He remembered trying to take a bite out of one of them and being shocked when he'd discovered it was plastic.

The realization hit him like a two-ton runaway truck.

Plastic? This tree stump was *fake*?

He gazed around him once more, his heart racing as it slowly dawned on him that everything he was seeing in this world, *everything*, was made of plastic. He touched the trees, the flowers, all fake. He could feel a breeze, but the leaves on the trees didn't even rustle. The only thing that moved were the butterflies. He wondered if they might be fake, too, like those mechanical butterflies he'd seen online when he'd been shopping for new skateboards. He put down his boots and walked over to one of them, slowly flapping its wings as it sat on a fake flower. He reached out to touch it—

"Ouch!"

A sharp pain shot down his finger. He pulled it back quickly and looked close—a welt was starting to form. Since when did butterflies sting? His finger really hurt. He shook his hand out, trying to shake away the pain. The welt puffed up and turned red. Like a bee sting— he'd once gotten a bunch of those when he and his friends thought it would be a good idea to throw base- balls at a beehive. He remembered the painful welts all over his arms and neck, the swelling and itching. This sting felt worse than all of those put together.

Thankfully, it stopped hurting pretty fast, faster than a regular bee sting anyway. But as he looked at his fin- ger, he saw that the red welt was turning purple. The skin around the wound felt tight, like it was—*harden- ing*. It couldn't be forming a scar already, could it? The purple turned to a deep, dark gray. He touched the cal- lous surface forming on his skin—it was cold and hard like . . . *metal*.

Levi's heart raced, and he felt a knot of fear in the pit of his stomach. The butterfly was still fluttering, watching him. Its wings seemed to be changing color— the bright red and yellow and purple hues dissolving into dark gray, the same color as the welt on his finger. The wings seemed to change shape, the soft, graceful edges becoming bent and jagged. It was almost as if the butterfly was turning into metal as well.

The butterfly continued to watch him. Then Levi saw dozens of tiny red beams of light, flashing like lasers from its eyes.

A shiver crept up Levi's spine and curled around his neck, making him shudder. Fear whispered softly in his ear, as if the butterfly itself were speaking: *you're trapped.*

He backed away slowly while the butterflies began swooping around his head. They lit on the trees and flowers around him, their wings—no longer full of color—beating slowly. There was something definitely very *wrong* about them. The more frightened he felt, the calmer they appeared, as if they were just waiting—for *something*.

Levi walked faster and faster. He wished he had his skateboard! Then he was running, but still he didn't seem to be getting anywhere. The castle in the distance stayed very far away.

It was like he was running in a circle.

Or *on* a circle.

He stopped, panting. He stared down at the stones under his feet. He took a step, and another. He was moving forward and yet he wasn't. He suddenly thought of a circus performer he'd seen once, balancing on top of a huge ball. The performer ran, making the ball spin, but he didn't really go anywhere . . .

Levi started walking fast again, his feet too sore now to run. He couldn't remember where he'd left his boots. He'd put them down when he went to investigate the butterfly, so they must be by the tree stump. But when the tree stump came around again, they weren't there. He wondered if he should go and look for them—but he had no idea where to begin. No matter where he went, he didn't seem to get anywhere at all. The view ahead of him never changed. He wondered if it was real or just a picture, like a backdrop in a play.

He stopped walking. There was no point in walking anymore, he realized. It was clear that he wasn't moving forward. But perhaps if he went *backward*, he would somehow get back to the gates where he'd first started with the others. Maybe Xavier was still there. He *had* been having a lot of trouble making up his mind about which way to go. Levi could tell him what he'd discovered, that maybe the way through the storm was the right path after all.

He felt better, having a plan in mind. He turned and started walking back. Maybe he'd find his boots along the way. But the same thing happened. The view never changed. He never got any closer to where he'd started. There was no gate anymore.

He was trapped.

No, I can get out of this. Ruwach's not going to just leave me here, is he?

He wasn't so sure about Ruwach. After all, he still hadn't even seen the dude's face. Maybe he was some kind of evil spirit, disguised as a helpful guide, and it was his intention all along to trap him in this miserable place. Didn't evil things dwell in caves? Like trolls?

He's not a troll. Evan had been so sure about that. But what did a little kid know anyway?

"Okay, Ruwach, if you can hear me, which way do I go now?"

No answer. He looked down at his breastplate. It was dark. The orb didn't spin. He hit it a few times with his fist, to see if he could jump-start it. Nothing.

Mom, Dad . . .

Were they worried about him? Was his dad still at the Rec, waiting for him? Maybe they didn't even know he was missing. The sun hadn't moved—maybe the time wasn't passing back in his world. *His* world. He wondered if earth existed anymore. He wondered about the other kids, too, and which way they had gone. Were they stuck somewhere too?

As he stood there, thinking about what he could do next, he felt the ground under his feet shift. The tremor was slight but enough to grab his attention. He stood as still as possible, wondering if any movement might cause more trouble. Several seconds passed as he waited. For what, he had no idea.

Silence.

Maybe it was nothing. He raised one foot to take another step. But he couldn't move it. He looked down and gasped. His bare feet were slowly disappearing into the cobbled road, as the road itself melted away.

He raised his head and called out: "Help!"

But his plea echoed back to him, unanswered.

CHAPTER TEN

No Turning Back

Xavier braced himself, arms across his face, lips pursed, eyes closed, expecting to be deluged by flying sand as soon as he passed through the gate. It took him a moment to realize that nothing had happened. He opened his eyes and peeked through the opening in his crossed arms. When he finally put them down, he marveled at the fact that the ferocious wind did not touch him at all. The storm raged all around him, but he couldn't feel it.

Xavier was in the storm but he wasn't *in* the storm. *Levi,* he thought. He wished he could go back and tell him—tell him that this way had been the right way after all. But when he looked back, he saw that the gate was gone. He noticed that his breastplate was pulsing faintly, and the pulsing got faster depending on which way he faced. He turned in a circle until the pulsing became a steady beam of light, aimed at the ground just in front of his feet. He took a step that way. And another. The light continued to shine just a little bit ahead of him, pointing the way. He looked ahead—all he saw was wild, whirling sand. But as he took each step, making sure the light from his breastplate was steady and didn't blink or flash, he was able to stay in the calm air.

How is Levi doing? Xavier thought as he navigated through the storm. He wondered if he should have been more forceful about preventing Levi from taking the other route. But maybe Levi was okay, sitting up there at that fancy castle waiting for them, eating ice cream, like he said. Xavier supposed he would find out when he got there, *if* he got there. There didn't seem to be an end to this sand storm. He couldn't even glimpse the beautiful castle that had appeared through the wide gate.

Had he made the right choice?

All he knew for sure was this: there was no turning back now.

He kept going, watching for the pulsing of the breastplate to correct his course now and then. After a while it got sort of boring. He could see the sun at times through breaks in the sandstorm, a fuzzy white circle in the sky. He wondered if it was the same sun they had back in their world. But this sun didn't move at all, so it was impossible to know how much time had passed—or if time was even passing at all.

He thought of his parents—had they woken up yet? Did they know he and his brother were gone? He wondered how Evan was doing, in that gloomy town with the bossy girl with the big eyes—had they gotten to the castle yet? Were they eating ice cream too, waiting for him to show up?

Xavier couldn't remember the last time he had been really alone like this. It wasn't a great feeling. He wished they hadn't had to split up in the first place. Why did they have to go through all this crazy stuff to get to that castle? What were they supposed to do when they got there? Was there going to be a battle then?

Xavier hoped Ruwach would suddenly appear to provide some answers. Then he remembered the last thing the little guide had said before he disappeared:

You already have everything you need.

Xavier had to trust that that was true.

He took his next step into the light, and his foot sank in soft sand up to his ankle. He tugged it out and then took another step, but that foot began to sink slowly as well. It suddenly got much harder to pull up his feet to take more steps—each time his boots sank deeper and deeper, until he almost couldn't move at all. His heart raced, and his breath caught in his throat as he realized what he was walking in.

Quicksand.

———

Evan and Brianna walked silently along the dark street, which seemed to go on forever. Tall gloomy buildings rose up on both sides, their windows shuttered. They leaned inward, creaking eerily, as if about to pounce on whoever walked by. There was no moon in the sky, no stars either. The duo couldn't see what lay ahead of them. The only illumination came from the street lamps, which winked on one by one as Evan and Brianna approached. Their breastplates glowed faintly, the steady beams of light shining in little pools in front of their feet.

"Do you think anyone lives here?" Brianna asked, gazing up at the run-down buildings. "Zombies maybe?"

"There's no such thing as zombies," said Evan.

"I read a book about zombies," said Brianna. "They hide in abandoned old buildings like this, and then they jump out at you while you're walking by, minding your own business—"

"There's no such thing as zombies! You read too much."

"How would you know? You probably don't read at all, do you?"

"I do so!" Evan said, reddening. "Man, how did I end up in this awful place with a know-it-all girl? That Roach guy must hate me."

"Ruwach!" Brianna said with a huff. "You can't even pronounce his name!"

"Well, it's a weird name," Evan said sullenly. "I don't get this. We're supposed to be in a battle. This isn't a battle! I mean, what's the point?"

"What if there are zombies—"

"There aren't any zombies already! And if there were, what would we fight them with? We don't even have any weapons!"

"Ruwach said we have everything we need," said Brianna, sounding as though she were trying to convince herself more than Evan. "If something jumps out at us—we'll know what to do. Right?"

"Like what?"

"Like—I don't know yet. Trust the armor. That's what Ruwach said. And your brother—he said it too."

"So you're taking advice from Xavier now?"

"He seems smart," said Brianna with a small shrug.

"So you're saying I'm not smart?"

"No, I didn't say that! He's just older and he—probably knows more."

Evan shook his head, disgusted. "You're just like everyone else. You think that Xavier is so great. Well, believe me, if you had to live with him, you probably wouldn't think that."

Brianna sighed but didn't answer. They walked in silence awhile.

"Do you think Levi is okay?" Brianna's voice was softer, edged in worry.

"He's probably doing better than we are right now," Evan muttered.

"I don't know. Levi's instruction was pretty clear about the wide gate and all. I'm not sure it was such a good idea—"

"Well, *we* followed the instructions, and we aren't doing so well, are we? I mean, look at this place!"

"Yeah, it's pretty creepy," Brianna said. "At least it's not raining anymore."

"Wouldn't want to mess up your hair," Evan muttered under his breath.

"What did you say?"

"I said, 'It sure isn't a day at the fair,'" Evan said aloud. "Are you *sure* we're supposed to be going this way?"

"This is the way the armor is telling us to go," Brianna replied. They had already figured out that their breast-plates stopped blinking and remained steady when they were headed in the right direction.

"Do you see it yet?" Evan asked. "That castle? We've got to be getting close."

"I can't see it," Brianna said. "I can hardly see anything. My feet hurt! I need to sit down for a minute."

"Sit where?"

"There!" Brianna said, pointing to a street lamp that had just blinked on. "A bench!"

"I don't think we should stop," Evan said, looking suspiciously at the bench, as if it might be a trap.

"Just for a minute! I'm tired! The Book didn't say anything about not taking breaks, did it?"

"No—but it didn't say we could, either."

"See?" Brianna flounced onto the bench. "Finally. Look, nothing happened. I'm fine."

Evan hesitated, still unsure about the safety of the bench. But after a moment he sat down too.

"I miss my mom," he said. "And my dad. You?"

"I don't live with my mom and dad," Brianna said.

"You don't? How come? Are they dead?"

"No, they aren't dead. They just can't take care of me. Me and my sisters live with my nana and Grandpa Tony."

"Oh. Grandparents are cool," Evan said. "My grandpa made me a sweet shield and sword once. I mean, when I was a *kid*," he added. "He makes stuff like that. He built a tree house for my mom when she was little. When we go to their house we can still play in it." He said it as if hoping Brianna would be impressed.

She wasn't.

"Stellar," she said with a hint of sarcasm.

"We moved to the country so we could be closer to them," Evan added.

"Did you want to move?"

"Not really. I miss my friends. But it's nice having a house and a yard. *And* I have my own room now too."

Brianna sighed. "I wish I had my own room. I have to share with my sisters. They hardly give me any space since I'm the youngest."

"Yeah, I know what that's like. Being the youngest. No fun."

"You got that right."

They were silent a moment. Then Evan spoke again.

"I wonder what they're doing."

"Who?"

"My parents. Your sisters. Our—*people*. Do you think they're looking for us?"

Brianna shrugged. "My sisters probably aren't. They hardly know I'm alive. But Nana and Grandpa Tony . . ." She paused. "Maybe they don't know we're gone yet. I mean, how long have we been here?"

"I don't know. I can't tell."

"Me neither."

Evan looked up at the sky, suddenly nervous. They had to get to that castle, wherever it was. *Soon.* "We should go," he said. He stood up.

"Ahhh!" Brianna cried, startling him. He whipped around and saw that the bench had tilted like a teeter-totter, and Brianna's end was literally sinking into the pavement, like a ship going down in the sea.

"Take my hand!" Evan yelled. Brianna reached for Evan's hand, and he pulled her with all his might, making a growling sound with the effort. He thought he might pull her arm right out of the socket, but Brianna managed to push off and get free of the sinking bench. Together they watched it go down and disappear with a loud gurgle.

"What's happening?" Brianna gasped.

"I don't know. But I think we need to get out of here!"

They stumbled away as the hole in the ground widened, swallowing cobblestones and street lamps. It rumbled and groaned like a monster devouring a whole village. A building nearby began to shift, leaning in farther as the ground under it was eaten away.

"Run!" Evan said.

The two kids raced up the street, but the sinkhole followed them, widening so that whole buildings behind them began to crumble and crash into it. It was insatiable, gobbling up everything in its path. Evan and Brianna could barely keep ahead of it.

Suddenly their breastplates began to blink furiously. The kids stopped, turning in all directions until the blinking light became a steady beam—aimed straight at a tall building on the side of the street.

"It wants us to go that way!" Brianna shouted.

They ran to the building, but there was no door or even a window to climb through. Just a solid wall.

"Now what do we do?" Brianna asked, her voice as shaky as the ground under their feet. She covered her ears to block out the horrible, gurgling noises of buildings and roadways being sucked into the pit.

Evan leaned back to look up, searching for something to climb on or a window higher up. He noticed that the beam from his breastplate pointed up as well—straight up the wall.

Up the wall?

"We have to go up the wall," he said to Brianna.

"Up the wall? Are you crazy?" Brianna gasped.

"Why not? Spider-Man can do it!"

"You are not Spider-Man!"

Evan lifted his foot, and as he did he felt his boot vibrate, sending out long tendrils that stuck to the wall like—*like Spider-Man*, he thought. *Cool.* He took a big breath and lifted the other foot off the ground, placing it on the wall, so that his body was now parallel with the ground. He thought he might fall upside down and crack his head on the sidewalk—but he didn't. He was standing on the wall, looking straight ahead at the starless sky, his mouth dropping open in wonder.

Brianna's eyes were even wider than usual. "How did you *do* that?"

"The boots! Try them!" Evan shouted. The ground under Brianna's feet began to tremble violently. "Come on! Step on the wall! Or you'll fall in!"

She looked at him and nodded, breathing deeply. *This is like jumping in the puddle of water,* she thought. *What have I got to lose?* The breastplate lit up the wall in front of her as if to confirm that she was making the right decision. She jumped with both feet onto the wall, just as the ground under her fell away.

Her boots sprang to life, several tendrils shooting out and cementing her securely. She let out a half-laugh, half-gasp. Her boots gripped the wall like spider legs. She felt weightless, her own body defying gravity. *Maybe this is how astronauts feel,* she thought. She took a step—her boots released easily and then gripped the wall once more when she put her foot down. Evan began to run up the wall—he actually looked like an astronaut, his feet lifting and falling almost in slow motion. Brianna began to run after him, enjoying the sensation of the boots gripping and releasing.

"Stellar!" Brianna said under her breath. "Wait till I tell my sisters—"

"Uh oh . . ."

The building they were walking on started to shake and wobble.

"It's gonna go down!" shouted Evan. "Hurry!"

They raced up the wall as fast as their boots would carry them, rounding the corner to the roof, just as the whole building began to collapse under them with a terrifying roar.

CHAPTER ELEVEN

A Helping Hand

Levi was buried up to his waist in the thick soupy ground that was slowly hardening like concrete. His sinking had slowed, but he was now so far in that he had no hope of escape.

"Help!" he yelled as loud as he could. But his voice just bounced back to him, as if it had hit a wall. That didn't seem possible, unless there actually *were* walls around him, walls he couldn't even see. "Help me!" He shouted over and over, hoping against hope that some-one—Ruwach perhaps—would come to rescue him. His screams ricocheted back to him, unanswered.

Wide is the gate that leads to destruction . . .

He'd taken the wrong path. He knew that now. But surely Ruwach wouldn't just leave him here. Surely he would come and save him . . .

"Ruwach! Over here! Help me!" He paused, but there was still no answer but his own echoing voice. "I'm sorry, okay? I made a mistake! Please help!"

Levi heard nothing but the fluttering wings of the butterflies. More and more of them were landing on the flowers, lining the road on either side of him, watching calmly as he tried to get free. Butterflies—they didn't look much like butterflies anymore, with their dark, angular wings that looked like they'd been cut from pieces of metal . . .

Maribuntas.

His heartbeat quickened. Brianna's story about the horrible black bugs with the huge stingers came back to him suddenly. Maybe these things really *were* Maribuntas—maybe they really existed.

"Someone help me!" Levi called out with fresh determination.

"Hello?"

Levi looked around, certain he had heard a voice. It had been very faint . . . perhaps he was imagining it. But then he saw something coming through the trees, *someone*, walking toward him. A kid.

"Xavier? Evan? Is that you?" he called out. He couldn't see the boy well at first, but there was something familiar about the way he moved, the way he was dressed. As he got closer, Levi could make out a Tony Hawk design on his T-shirt. It was the same as his own shirt—the one he'd been wearing at the Rec before grabbing the Crest and being sucked into this world. Maybe there was another kid from the Rec here, someone who'd come through after him—and he was here in this plastic dome with him. Or maybe Ruwach had sent someone here—to rescue him!

Hope welled up in Levi's heart as the kid came toward him, strolling along as if he had all the time in the world. The kid was carrying a skateboard. Awesome! They could take turns riding it, maybe find a way out of this place.

But as the other kid came into focus, Levi began to get confused. He blinked several times—the image he was seeing couldn't be right. He balled up his fists and rubbed his eyes, then looked again. Something was wrong with his vision, certainly. It must be a dream, or maybe he was just seeing things after being stuck here in this crazy world for so long. Because what he was seeing was simply impossible.

This kid looked *exactly* like Levi himself.

Levi stared, unbelieving, at this *other* Levi. His face, his clothes, his cool Vans, everything about him was the same. Even the birthmark on the left side of his neck—*his* birthmark! He opened his mouth to speak, but nothing came out. It couldn't. It *wouldn't*. He was looking at a mirror image of . . . himself.

Other Levi stopped and was looking at him curiously. "Hey, man, you in a jam?"

It even sounded like him! Levi's mouth opened and closed like a fish. Other Levi walked over to him and set the skateboard down.

"Can you talk?" asked Other Levi, a half-smile curving his face. Levi's smile, chipped tooth and all.

"Yeah," Levi said finally, swallowing. His mouth was very dry. The shock of seeing himself—or a clone of himself—had made him momentarily forget that he was still stuck in the ground. "But who are—how did you—?"

Other Levi crouched down, examining the situation. "Whoa. You need to get out of there, man. Can I give you a hand?" Other Levi stretched out his hand. "Here, grab on. I'll pull you out."

Levi stared at the outstretched arm—*his* arm—with the same scar on his forearm he had gotten in a skateboard accident when he was seven. But it couldn't be *him*, could it? He was convinced that he was hallucinating.

Wide is the gate that leads to destruction . . .

Levi didn't know Ruwach very well, but he had a feeling that this was not how Ruwach would rescue him, if he decided to rescue him at all. Something about this seemed too easy, too convenient. But Levi didn't think he had much of a choice. There was no way he was getting out of this mess if he didn't accept this Other Levi's help. He took a breath and reached out his arm.

Other Levi grabbed his hand. His grip was strong—and cold.

"Pull me up!" Levi shouted, using his other hand to get some leverage on the edge of the sinkhole. "Pull me up!"

But Other Levi didn't pull him up. He stood frozen, his hand locked on Levi's. With mounting horror, Levi saw that the clone's hand was changing. Hardening. A grayness encompassed the clone's fingertips, spreading down to his palm and wrist. *It was turning to metal, just like the butterflies had.* And the gray from the clone was now spreading to Levi's own hand.

He frantically tried to make the clone release its grip, but it was locked on tight. He pulled and pulled, but the more he struggled, the faster the gray metallic coating spread up his arm. So, he forced himself to be still. He watched Other Levi rapidly changing, its arms and legs becoming wrapped in metal plates held together with rivets, its face disappearing behind an iron mask. Any human features it once had soon morphed into mechanized parts. Its eyes—now just red glowing orbs like the butterflies'—stared at Levi, pulsing with intensity, as if willing Levi's body to change along with it.

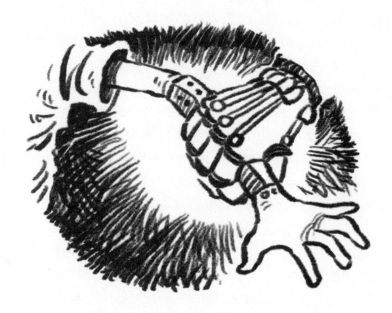

Levi watched as the gray metal crept up his arm—slowly, steadily. Eventually, he thought, it would cover his whole body. He would look exactly like this ghastly metal thing that held him fast. And there was nothing he could do about it.

"Ruwach!" he called out desperately. "Somebody! Help me!"

Again the words echoed back to his own ears, unanswered.

———

Xavier pedaled his feet in the quickening sand, trying to get enough leverage to stay above ground. It was hard, desperate work, but somehow he managed to push himself up far enough to get one knee above the sand. He crawled out and sprawled on the ground, gasping for breath. That was close. *Too* close. He lay still a moment, letting the hammering of his heart diminish a little. But soon he felt the sand under him start to give way again. He quickly rolled over and crab-walked away before a second patch of quicksand collapsed under him. He wondered if the armor had led him into a trap.

He glanced down at his breastplate, which was flickering, the orb spinning, the words becoming visible: *Follow the Way of the Armor. It will lead you . . .*

"Okay, lead me," he said aloud. As if in answer to his request, the breastplate focused a beam of light at a space just ahead of him in the shifting sand. Xavier stared at the spot a moment, uncertain. He didn't see how that particular spot was any safer than where he was right now. But he'd asked, and the armor had answered. He struggled to his feet and leaped to that space, half-expecting to be sucked down into the sand once again. But that didn't happen. Somehow, he was standing on solid ground that looked anything but solid. He gazed down at his feet, amazed.

Another spot lit up a couple of feet away. Xavier held his breath and leaped again, just making it into the lighted spot. It was solid. Around him the sand was churning, undulating, like waves on the ocean, but wherever the light was, the ground was solid and unmoving.

Another light, this one a little farther away. Xavier swung his arms for extra momentum and leaped again—he didn't think he would make it, but somehow he did. It was like jumping from stone to stone in a streambed, only each time the little "stones" of light got farther away. He had to leap farther, and although he didn't think he would be able to do it, he always made it to the next spot.

After about ten leaps, the lights suddenly stopped, and the breastplate went dark. Xavier stood on the last spot of light, unsure what to do. His heart raced as he watched the sand continue to drop away around him. He rapped on the breastplate, trying to get it working again. Nothing happened. Frustrated, he almost tore it off and threw it away—but he couldn't dislodge it from his shirt.

Behind him the ground had all but collapsed into a dark void. The desert ahead of him continued to roll and churn like a storm at sea.

It will lead you . . . It WILL . . .

I just have to wait, Xavier thought. *Be patient. Wait. It will lead me, it will lead me . . .*

He chanted those words over and over to himself, trying not to think about the collapsing ground behind him, the roiling sand ahead of him. The spot under his feet was still solid, at least for now. He wondered how long it would hold up.

Follow the Way of the Armor . . .

He closed his eyes so he wouldn't have to look at the storm anymore. He tried to think about something else. Home, his parents, school starting next week. School— it seemed like a million miles away now. He wondered if he would ever get there. Would he go back to his world again? He'd been nervous about starting at a new school. But that was nothing compared to what he'd been going through since he came to Ahoratos.

Ahoratos. Ruwach had said there would be battles, but this was not the sort of battle he had thought he would face. So far the enemy had been falling trees, lightning, sandstorms—and his own doubts and fears. It didn't feel like a fair fight. It certainly wasn't like the battles he had read about, or acted out with his brother, or played in video games. There the enemy was always some terrible monster or dragon or black knight on a horse. Those kinds of enemies were so much easier to recognize, to fight. But this—this was *way* harder.

Xavier's ears perked up. He heard something. Something new, something different from the constant whine of the sandstorm. It sounded like—laughter.

His eyes flicked open and gazed out into the blowing sand—the storm seemed to be clearing, like a window unfogging. He could make out a scene—a group of people. Levi! And Evan! And Brianna! They were sitting at a huge table filled with food of all kinds, a banquet fit for a king. Or several kings. They were eating and talking happily. The room around them was very grand, like the feasting hall of a castle. Then Xavier's vision zoomed out, to the outside of the castle, and then farther still, to the whole kingdom, the mountains, the valleys, the trees, and the streams. There it was!

A path appeared in front of him, a series of stepping stones leading the way through the churning sand to the vision of the city. That was it! The clear path! It was only a few steps away. Soon he'd be in the castle, with his friends and his brother, stuffing himself with that wonderful food. He realized then just how hungry and thirsty he was.

He was about to leap onto the first stone when something made him hesitate just long enough for Ruwach's words to resonate in his heart.

Follow the Way of the Armor.

He looked down at his breastplate. It was still dark.

He tapped it again. Was it even on? Maybe the batteries were dead. Ruwach hadn't mentioned having to recharge it.

The orb glowed faintly, the words spilling out into the air in front of him.

> *Guard your heart above all else,*
>
> *for it determines your path.*

His heart wanted to leap down the stone path to the castle. To reunite with his brother and his new friends. But the breastplate was not giving him permission.

"Come on! Say something!" he said irritably, tapping it harder. He looked up at the scene of food and friends in front of him, then back down at the breastplate. Still nothing.

Just wait.

Xavier waited.

It will lead you down the right path . . .

Frustrated, Xavier threw back his head, looking up toward the sky as he let out a long sigh. His body was angled back just enough for the breastplate to tilt upward. In that moment it lit up like it was set on fire, emitting a brilliant white beam of light. But it wasn't directed at the sand before him. It was aimed upward.

Xavier's eyes followed the light beam to a tall cliff appearing through the sandstorm—at least thirty feet high.

Seriously? You want me to jump . . . up there? he thought to himself.

The beam was steady on the cliff's ledge. It would take superpowers to get to that ledge in one jump. He'd never make it. He shuddered as he considered the consequences: falling into an endless pit? Being buried in sand? He looked again at the scene of the beautiful kingdom, waiting before him. Then he remembered Levi and the wide gate. How inviting and real it had appeared.

Lean not on your own understanding.

He sighed to himself. *Only one way to find out.*

He started to lift one foot off the ground, but his boots felt funny. He looked down and saw a faint reddish glow around the soles of his feet. The bottom of his feet felt very warm. The glow intensified—he thought he saw a flame sprout from the heels.

Jump.

He looked up again at the ledge. *Here goes nothing.*

He crouched down, took a deep breath, and jumped.

The boots seemed to launch him into the air. *I could use these on the basketball court,* he thought as he soared easily up to the top of the cliff. Below him, the sandstorm and the entire desert disappeared from view. He sailed toward the cliff where the light from his breastplate shone.

In a moment he landed gently, like he'd been set down by some friendly giant. He was standing on grass in a sunny meadow. No more sand. The sky was blue. A soft wind caressed his face. It was like he'd jumped into a new world completely. A world of peace and rest. Like summer vacation. He took a deep breath. And then another.

He straightened, gazing around him. The land sloped down to a streambed edged in tall grass and wildflowers. Big lazy willows leaned over the stream, dipping their long branches into the water. Xavier remembered how thirsty he was. He loped down the hill to the water, knelt, and scooped up a handful into his mouth. The water was clear and cold, delicious. He drank as much as he could and then lay back in the grass, basking in the shade of the willows. A little rest was all he needed. He'd made it out of the sandstorm. Not too much farther now, he was sure of it. Around him butterflies flitted lazily. Lots and lots of butterflies. He smiled, his eyes feeling heavy. Heavier than they'd ever felt. *Maybe a nap,* he thought.

Just a quick one . . .

CHAPTER TWELVE

Butterfly Kisses

*W*e're going to fall!"

Brianna yelled to Evan as they hoisted themselves over the top ledge of the building, which had begun to collapse under them.

But they didn't fall. The roof didn't collapse. In fact, it wasn't even a roof.

It was another landscape altogether. A meadow.

The two exhausted kids sat up and gazed around them at the waves of tall grass and flowers spread in riotous color all the way to the edge of a thick forest. No more crashing buildings, no more sinkholes. All was quiet, the only sound a soft breeze bending the flowers, wafting across their fevered faces. They blinked and stared, unable to get their bearings for a long moment.

"Where are we?" Brianna asked softly.

"I . . . don't . . . know . . ." Evan murmured.

Brianna reached out a cautious hand toward the ground, feeling around to see if it was solid. Evan did the same thing, making sure that what they were sitting on was going to stay there.

"Feels . . . okay," he said after a moment.

Brianna touched one of the flowers with the tip of her finger, then tilted it to her nose. It smelled glorious.

"Stellar," she said. A butterfly landed on a flower, and she jumped at the sudden movement, half-expecting something to fall on her. She almost laughed when she saw it was only a butterfly.

Evan kept looking around, also expecting something awful to happen any moment. He was still trying to figure it all out. "So we climbed up to the roof—and we landed here. So the roof of that building was like a—portal?"

"Yeah, guess so."

Another butterfly landed near the first one. They were much bigger than normal butterflies with wildly colorful wings that glittered in the sun. Brianna smiled, relaxing. She reached out to touch them, sure they would fly away. But they didn't.

Evan was still curious as to how they'd managed to climb up a wall. He lifted up one foot to examine the boot. It looked the same as before. There was no evidence of spikes or claws or suction cups or anything that would make them stick to a wall.

"How did these boots do that?" Evan said, more or less to himself.

"They're magic boots!" Brianna said, her attention still captivated by the butterflies.

"Yeah . . . Ru said we'd have everything we needed. He's full of surprises, that guy."

Brianna didn't answer. She was making goo-goo eyes at the butterflies.

"Hey, we need to get moving," Evan said, annoyed that she was not really listening to him. "I'm getting hungry."

Brianna finally did look at him, as if just realizing he was still there. "Yeah, me too, come to think of it. And thirsty."

"I could go for a grape soda."

"Grape soda!" Brianna rolled her eyes. "I could go for a big glass of lemonade—"

More butterflies floated toward them, their glittery wings sparkling as they landed on the wildflowers surrounding them.

"Glitter butterflies? No way," Evan said, horrified. "They must be—what do you call them—hallelujahs?"

"Hallucinations?" said Brianna, shaking her head. "But these are real. And so pretty!" She leaned in toward the one closest to her. "Hello there, beautiful butterfly. What's your name?"

"Oh please," Evan said. "She's talking to butterflies now." He looked suspiciously at the butterflies. There was something definitely not normal about them. They were as big as birds, and they had a way of—staring—that made him very uneasy. It wasn't too surprising, after all, since pretty much everything was different here than on earth.

"Hey, I don't think we should be messing with those," Evan said, standing up. "We should keep going."

"Who says?" asked Brianna, sounding annoyed.

"You know what happened the last time we took a break—"

"Oh relax, Evan. You're such a worrywart. We don't even have any direction from the armor yet."

"This way," said a soft voice, delicate and sweet as honey. Evan looked around.

"Did you say that?" he asked.

Brianna shook her head. She hesitated, not sure if she should say what she was thinking, because she wasn't sure how it could be possible. "I think—it was the *butterfly*—I think it talked." Brianna stared at the butterfly, moving a few steps closer.

"Follow me." The butterfly flapped its wings, lifted off the flower, and flew a short distance away. It landed on another flower, as if waiting for her to follow. The others followed its lead, filling the whole meadow with glorious color like a moving carpet.

"It talked—did you hear it?" Brianna gulped hard. Never had she imagined, even with her *own* wild imagination, that anything so marvelous could really happen.

"No way," said Evan. But he had heard it too, and it made him even more anxious. "Don't listen to it. We have to wait for the armor—"

But Brianna didn't seem to hear him at all. She had scampered after the butterflies, which continued to fly away and land again, just out of reach. She gasped with delight as she chased them all the way to the edge of the forest.

"Come back!" Evan shouted. He chased after her, calling to her to stop. She paid no attention.

Evan's breastplate began to blink. He stopped running after Brianna and began turning in a circle until the light stopped blinking and became steady. It was pointed in the exact *opposite* direction of where Brianna was headed.

"Hey! Look! We need to go this way!" he called to Brianna, who was now farther away, headed into the woods. "That's not the way!"

It was too late. She was already gone.

"She never listens!" Evan said to himself. He looked from his breastplate and then to the woods. Should he go off on his own or go after her? He couldn't leave her alone. Who knew what sort of trouble she would get herself into? He sighed and turned away from the right path, heading into the trees after Brianna.

It was so dark in the woods he couldn't even see the sky anymore. The trees were tall, with black, evil-looking leaves that reminded him of the forest he and Xavier first ran through to get to the Cave. There was no sound. The leaves didn't rustle. No birds sang either.

The strange butterflies perched on saplings and low branches, lined up like little soldiers. They did not look colorful here—their wings had changed to a dull, metallic gray. They glared at him with red, glowing eyes, beating their wings slowly. Evan took a deep breath and kept walking, searching for Brianna.

After a while, he saw her. She was sitting on a tree stump with a lazy grin on her face, her gaze fixed on that same huge butterfly (or whatever it was) she'd been chasing. Apparently she didn't even notice that it was no longer glittery. Its red eyes were locked on hers, as if it were controlling her with its laserlike gaze. She seemed to be carrying on a happy conversation that only the two of them could hear.

"Brianna!" he called over to her. She whirled around to face him and all the butterflies did too, fixing their beady red eyes on him. It was like they *heard* him, could understand what he was saying. He felt unnerved by their eerie stares.

"Hey, Evan! Come say hello to my new friend," Brianna said, waving to him as he came closer.

"Brianna, the armor says we need to go—*that* way," Evan said, pointing out of the forest.

"Just a few more minutes! Eleanor was just telling me the most wonderful story . . ."

"Eleanor?"

"That's her name! It's like my favorite name in the whole world. I wish *my* name was Eleanor—"

"Brianna, that butterfly—it's not even a butterfly! You need to get away from it right now—"

"Don't be silly, Evan. She's the sweetest thing. Come over and meet her—"

Brianna's head was turned toward Evan, so she didn't see her sweet little butterfly, the one that had led her to this place, open its wings and rise up into the air. Evan stared aghast at its large gray body, segmented as if it were armored, and its long tail. Wait a minute—butterflies didn't have tails, did they? The thick tail curled toward Brianna, and Evan realized it wasn't a tail at all—it was a *stinger*. He blinked, shocked by what he was seeing. Butterflies weren't supposed to have stingers either! Evan started to run toward Brianna, shouting as he went.

"Look out!" He ran as fast as his boots would carry him.

"What's the matter?" Brianna turned to look at her beloved butterfly—her eyes widened in alarm.

She realized all at once what it was. "Maribunta!" she shrieked.

"Eleanor" made a noise like a cackle and shot a thin, silver, javelinlike dart at Brianna. Before he even knew what he was doing, Evan threw himself in front of her. He shut his eyes, bracing for the impact of the deadly dart in the middle of his chest.

"Evan!" Brianna cried.

Evan heard a clang and felt a jolt as the dart knocked him backward. He sprawled on the ground and lay still, wondering if he was still alive. He took a breath. Then another. Apparently he was. But was he wounded? He opened his eyes, looking down at his chest with a wince. The dart wasn't there—it had bounced off his breastplate and ricocheted into a nearby tree. He almost laughed out of sheer gratitude—the breastplate had actually guarded his heart.

Brianna rushed over to help him. "Quick! There!" she whispered, indicating a leafy bush. She quickly helped him to his feet, and the two of them dove into it, covering their heads and staying as still as possible.

The evil Eleanor creature was angry—it made a hideous screeching sound, calling the other butterfly things to attention. Brianna peeked out to see a whole bunch of them swarming together, their red laser eyes scanning the forest, their long antennae probing the air.

"What are they doing?" Evan asked in a hoarse whisper.

"Looking for us." Brianna peered through the leaves. "I read somewhere that butterflies can't see well in the dark. But they can hear . . . with their antennae." She put a finger to her lips. The two kids stayed as quiet as they possibly could as the Maribuntas continued to search for them.

Brianna was just beginning to wonder how long they could stay perfectly still when her breastplate began to pulse softly. Evan's did too.

"What's it doing?" Evan whispered.

"I'm not sure." Brianna couldn't see any light coming from the breastplate, but she could feel subtle, sound-less vibrations. Then she thought she understood. She whispered, "It's telling us which way to go—without telling *them* which way we will go."

Evan understood.

The two kids began to shift their positions in the bush until the vibrations stopped. Evan raised one finger and pointed in that direction. She nodded, understanding. Evan couldn't see any path before him, just black forest, but he thought he heard Ruwach's voice somewhere—up in the treetops perhaps? *You already have everything you need.* He took a deep breath. *This better work.* He held up three fingers so Brianna could see his count. He took another breath. Then he lowered one finger, then the next, then the last.

The two kids jumped up from their hiding place and ran. The Maribuntas, alerted by their movement, raced after them. Brianna grabbed Evan's hand as they tumbled over twigs and brush, keeping their heads down as best they could. Deadly darts sailed past them on all sides, some just inches away from their heads. They kept on running until Brianna spotted a bright splash of sunlight peeking through the dense trees.

"There!" she cried.

They ran toward the light, finally crashing through dense undergrowth into tall, bright grass. They fell forward and lay still, breathing hard, waiting for the angry insects to zero in on them with their evil stingers. But it was quiet.

Brianna was the first to take a peek. She saw only pretty, sparkly butterflies fluttering among the wildflowers at the edge of the forest.

"Where'd they go?" said Evan, still panting from the ordeal.

"I don't know. It's like they changed back . . . into butterflies . . ." Brianna couldn't even finish.

They sat in the cool grass a long moment, trying to get their breath. Evan thought his heart might explode out of his chest; it was beating so fast. Sweat dripped down the side of his face. He wiped it away.

"That was close," he said.

He glanced over at Brianna, surprised to see her big eyes all watery, like they were filling with tears.

"I'm sorry." She sniffed, wiping at her eyes with the back of her hand. "I'm so sorry. I didn't mean—"

"Yeah, yeah, I know," Evan said. Nothing made him more uncomfortable than seeing a girl cry.

"Thank you, Evan—for coming for me."

"It's okay."

Then Brianna did something truly horrifying. She hugged him.

"Yuck!" he said, pushing her away. "Don't *ever* do that again!"

"Oh, sorry, I was just trying to say thanks," she said, deflated.

"Don't thank me, thank Ru," said Evan. "He gave us the armor. But no more chasing butterflies, capeesh?"

"*Capeesh?* What's that mean?"

"Uh—nothing." Evan stood up, brushing off his pants. "What did you call those things? Mariachis?"

"Maribuntas," Brianna said. She thought about the story she'd told Landon about the *Lupinas Ala Maribunta*. Big black bugs with stingers the size of ballpoint pens. "I didn't think they really existed."

Their breastplates began to blink again. Evan swiveled around until the light became steady.

"Come on," he said. "We need to keep going."

"There's no path!"

"It doesn't matter. This is the way the armor is pointing. So we're going."

They made their way through the tall grass, searching for a clear path. The meadow seemed endless. But then the ground began to slope downward, which made the going easier. Evan could make out a wide stream below—cool, inviting water tumbling softly over pebbles. And then he saw something else—something that made his heart nearly burst.

"Look!" he shouted. "There's my brother!"

CHAPTER THIRTEEN

The Water Rises

Xavier awoke to the sound of a familiar voice. He sat up, blinking, trying to shake the sleep from his head. He wasn't sure how long he'd been out.

"Xavi!"

He looked up to see his brother running down the hill toward him. Brianna was close behind. They looked like they were okay. He stood up, overjoyed to see them. He realized he was standing in water—it was seeping into the ventilation slats of his boots. The water in the stream must have risen while he was asleep. He took a few steps up the bank toward his brother.

"Evan! Brianna! How'd you find me?"

They both began talking at once, telling an incredible story—something about walking on walls and big ugly bugs. When Brianna told him about how Evan had come to rescue her, he turned to his little brother with genuine admiration on his face. "Way to go."

"It was no big deal," Evan said, hanging his head to hide his wide grin.

"Have you seen Levi?" Brianna asked. "Is he here?"

"I haven't seen him," Xavier told her.

"Maybe he made it to the castle already," she said hopefully.

"Is that real water?" Evan asked, pointing to the stream. "I am so thirsty."

"Yeah, help yourself," said Xavier. "But be careful, the water's rising pretty fast."

Evan and Brianna both knelt down by the stream. Brianna dipped her hand in daintily, but Evan used both hands, splashing his whole face and laughing.

"Evan, you're splashing me," Brianna said, annoyed.

"Can't help it! Almost as good as grape soda," Evan said, relishing every drop.

"It's not anything like grape soda," she said, rolling her eyes.

While they drank, Xavier told them what had happened to him and how he had gotten to the stream. They were amazed at his story, so different from theirs but then again sort of similar.

"Your boots became jet boots?" Evan said, awestruck. "I want jet boots!"

"Our boots walked on walls, Evan," Brianna reminded him. "Isn't that cool enough for you?"

"Jet boots would have been faster," Evan said. "We could have flown all the way to the top instead of walking."

Brianna threw her arms in the air. "So what happened next?" She turned to Xavier, clearly more enthralled with his story than Evan was.

"And then I fell asleep," Xavier said. "I'm not sure how long I've been asleep here." He looked at the stream—water pooled around his boots. "We should move back up the hill." His breastplate began to blink rapidly. That always meant: *time to go.*

"I'm not done!" Evan said, still splashing himself with water. "What's the hurry anyway? We just escaped from a swarm of giant Mangobugs, or whatever you call them. We need a break."

"It *was* pretty exhausting," Brianna said with a huge yawn. "Gosh, I didn't realize how tired I was." She lay back on the grassy bank, sighing deeply.

"Me neither," said Evan. "Saving your life took a lot out of me."

"It's really nice here," said Brianna in a sleepy voice.

"You guys, we can't stay here," Xavier insisted. "You need to get up!"

"I know, I know," said Brianna. "But I don't think I can do it. I'm too tired. Just for a minute, okay?"

"No, it's not okay!" Xavier said.

"Yeah—we need to go," said Evan. He tried to get up, but he felt something heavy on his eyelids, something that seemed to push him back down to the soft, cool grass again. He reached up to brush it away—but it stayed there, like the big soft fleece blanket on his bed at home, settling over him, forcing his eyes closed. "We . . . need . . . to . . . go . . ." Evan fell back on the grass, sound asleep.

"Get up, guys!" Xavier shouted. He tugged on Evan's arm to no avail. "Wake up!" It did no good. The water kept rising, lapping at their legs.

Xavier wondered if it was the water that made them so sleepy—after all, he had gotten sleepy after drinking it too. For the first time he realized that this cool, refreshing stream may not be the safe haven he had believed it to be.

Then he heard a noise, like the beginning of thunder. But it didn't end like thunder usually did. It kept going, getting louder and louder. He gazed upstream and saw that the water was not only getting higher, but the current was moving even faster, forming whitecaps as it sped over rocks and around boulders. It was weird how fast this was happening, but then again, this was the way things seemed to go in Ahoratos. Xavier knew he wasn't dreaming this time.

The rumble became a roar. Xavier looked upstream and saw a wall of water rising up, headed straight for them as if a dam had broken. The water thundered as it raced down the creek bed, collapsing the banks and consuming plants and trees on either side.

Xavier felt a pit open up in the center of his stomach as he watched the water head right for them. He looked up the bank—he doubted it was high enough to avoid the water, even if he could get these two kids all the way up there. There was no time to even try.

Xavier tried shaking them awake again. Neither one even fluttered an eyelid. It was like they were in some sort of trance. If he didn't do something fast, all three of them were going to get swept away.

Xavier wondered if Ruwach had known this would happen. "You have an enemy," he had said. "An enemy who will use any means to distract you, to discourage you, to delay you, to defeat you." If this was the work of this enemy, then Xavier had to figure out a way to overcome it. And quickly.

If he could somehow keep them together, perhaps they could ride out the wave. But with what? He looked around frantically for a long vine or a rope—a rope? There wasn't any rope. All he had was—a belt.

The belt holds everything together. Ruwach's words replayed in his mind.

He reached down, grasped his belt in both hands, and pulled it apart. Even though he couldn't even see where it was joined, the belt came off easily. It wasn't long enough, but perhaps if he could stretch it, he could get it around the three of them. It was nearly hopeless, but it was all he could think to do. He quickly looped the belt under the two sleepers, then lay down between them, grasped the two ends, and pulled them together over all three of their bodies. The belt strained and stretched as Xavier pulled both ends together, and to his relief, he got them to touch. They fused together, tightening securely around all three, creating a little human bundle. Xavier put his arms around Evan and Brianna and shut his eyes, bracing for the impact.

The wall of water slammed into them with a mighty roar. Xavier felt as though he were being shot from a cannon, like a clown at the circus. The force of the water was so strong it knocked out his breath. He kept a tight hold on his companions as the surging water swept them downstream. He thought they would be dragged under, but instead he felt as though they were actually being lifted, floating on top of the water. He opened his eyes, unable to make out anything but the relentless waves thrashing against him. He coughed and gagged, searching for air. Then he realized that something was surrounding them, compressing them, protecting them from the force of the water. He looked down to see that the belt had *inflated* around them like an inner tube. They were going on the wildest tube ride of their lives.

They bounced and jetted over the turbulent water, which spun them around eddies and hurled them into boulders. At one point, they hit a large rock and catapulted straight into the air. Xavier felt his stomach lurch into his throat, but the tube prevented them from getting bruised. They ricocheted through a chute and cartwheeled several times, making Xavier dizzy. No sooner had they landed than the water swept them away again, faster and faster. The water stung Xavier's eyes and pounded his face and arms, but he kept a tight hold on the two sleeping kids and worked frantically to keep their heads above water. Nothing about the situation was sure, except one thing: the tube kept them strapped together securely.

Too bad Evan is missing this, Xavier thought. They'd been white-water rafting once on a camping trip, but that was nothing compared to this. It would have been fun if it weren't so terrifying. He wondered if this ride would ever end.

Instead of slowing down, Xavier sensed the current getting even stronger. He was able to turn his head in time to see what they were headed for.

Waterfall.

"Hang on!" he whispered, as much to himself as to the others, even though they were still asleep. He closed his eyes and held on tight.

They plunged over the lip of the waterfall, and Xavier felt suspended for a split second, like the cartoon animals do when they run off a cliff but don't realize it. Then the falling water caught them, hurtling them toward the unknown below. Xavier's stomach took up residence in his throat. *This is like the flume ride at Six Flags,* he told himself. Except he wasn't sure that they'd make it out of this ride alive.

"Ahhhh!" As if on cue, both Evan and Brianna woke up suddenly as their makeshift raft careened down the waterfall.

"Hang on and hold your breath!" was all Xavier could say as water pummeled them, drowning out any more words.

It was over in seconds—yet it seemed like a million years.

They hit the water like a meteor, then plummeted under for a few heart-stopping seconds before bobbing up to the surface again. They wobbled a bit as the water smoothed out, finally calm.

"What's happening?" Brianna said, coughing up mouthfuls of water.

"Yeah, what was that?" croaked Evan. "I thought we were . . . I thought . . ."

"Waterfall," Xavier said, barely able to catch his breath. His heart pounded still. "We just went over . . . a waterfall."

"Waterfall! Why didn't you wake me up?" Evan exclaimed.

"I tried. Are you guys okay?"

"I think so," said Brianna. "But where'd this raft thing come from?"

"You're probably not going to believe it."

It will lead you down the right path. The instruction never said it would be a *calm* path, or an *easy* path. Just the *right* path.

"We're okay now." Xavier saw a beach ahead and began kicking toward it. The raft deflated as soon as his feet touched the sandy bottom. Xavier pulled it apart and the three of them separated, splashing around to get their footing. They felt dizzy and waterlogged from the crazy ride. Xavier shook his head to get the water out of his ears. Brianna and Evan stumbled toward the beach and collapsed.

Xavier buckled his belt back on, still amazed at what it had done. It fit his waist perfectly again. He sat down on the sand, lowering his head to stop the spinning.

"I thought I was dreaming," Brianna said.

"You were, for a while," said Xavier. "For most of the ride down the river, I couldn't wake either of you up."

"Ride? Down the river?" Brianna asked, her eyes wide.

"Why were we so sleepy?" said Evan.

"The water you drank," Xavier said. "I think it made you sleepy. Maybe it was one of those enemy attacks Ruwach told us about."

"This enemy sure doesn't attack like a normal enemy," Brianna said.

"Isn't that what Ruwach was trying to tell us?" Evan asked. "Well, a little warning would have been nice."

"Maybe it's just something—we always have to be on alert for," said Xavier thoughtfully.

"Where are we anyway?" said Evan. He had recovered himself enough to start looking around.

"I think—we're there." Xavier pointed behind them. Evan and Brianna both turned to look, their mouths dropping open in unison.

Above them, perched on a ring of clouds, sat the magnificent castle they had seen only from a distance, bathed in ethereal sunlight so it glimmered like something not quite real. The castle seemed to go on forever, its many turrets and towers looking more like sleek white peaks cutting into the sky, smooth as ice. The air around the castle was filled with small flickering lights, like the ones they had seen in the Cave.

"It's so . . . beautiful," breathed Brianna.

"Yeah, but how do we get up there?" Evan asked.

There didn't seem to be any sort of path.

Ruwach's familiar voice interrupted their musing. "Well done, Warriors."

All three kids turned, and there he was, standing there as if he'd just come out of the water. He looked bigger than he had in the Cave, and there seemed to be something visible beneath the dark hood. Xavier wondered if he was catching a glimpse of Ruwach's nose.

"Ruwach!" Xavier said. "Where did you—?"

"Are we glad to see you!" Brianna said, interrupting. "Is Levi up there? Did he make it?"

Ruwach shook his head slowly. "I'm afraid not. Levi is—trapped."

"Trapped?"

"He chose the wrong path. And the wrong path always leads to disaster." Ruwach leaned toward Brianna and Evan when he spoke, as if he wasn't just referring to Levi alone.

"Well, can't you just go and get him?" Brianna demanded, stamping her foot. "Don't you have magic powers or something?"

"I'm afraid that is not how it works," said Ruwach, with genuine sorrow in his voice. "But he is safe for the moment. I have made sure of that. Come to the castle, have something to eat, and we will talk about what has to be done. There is someone there waiting for you."

Ruwach pointed with his long draped arm toward the castle. The kids turned and were surprised to see a magnificent staircase leading from the beach to the castle. Each step flickered unsteadily, as if it were made of light.

"Where'd that come from?" said Evan. "It wasn't there a minute ago."

"Follow me," said Ruwach, gliding up the shining steps.

Brianna hesitated. "Is it safe?" she asked, suspicious.

Ruwach stopped, his hooded head turning slowly to face her. Then his shoulders moved up and down in what could only have been a sort of chuckle.

"Safe?" he said, a sudden lightness in his tone. "It may or may not be safe, but it will most definitely be worth it."

CHAPTER FOURTEEN

Castle in the Air

Xavier stepped carefully onto the stairway of light, followed by Evan and Brianna. It held them despite its transparency. None of them commented—by this time they had stopped being surprised by much of anything.

They trudged up the steps, their joy at finally reaching their destination dampened by the absence of Levi. When they emerged from the cloud layer, they found themselves on a grand balcony of smooth, marble-like, white stone, overlooking the lake. A giant gate stood before them, leading into the castle. It glittered as if crusted with thousands of diamonds, making it almost hard to look at in the bright sun. The little puffs of light darted around them, sparkling like brilliant gems. The very air seemed filled with starry light. The kids stared around them, unsure of what to make of it all.

Evan was the first to move, running to the edge of the balcony to view the kingdom spread out below them. The other two followed. From this vantage point, they could see that Ahoratos was bigger than they had first imagined, an endless landscape of mountains, forests, and rivers. But the mountains looked nothing like the mountains back home—they were tall and twisty, as if formed from cords of rock, and they were fringed by lacy trees and brilliant flowers. Waterfalls streamed from the faces of the mountains into a wide blue river that wound through the landscape, kissed by the golden light of the sun. Large lumpy objects, almost like rocks, hung in the golden sky. A fine mist drifted over the water and around the mountains, casting the whole scene in dreamy majesty.

"Whoa," said Evan. He couldn't think of anything else to say.

"What's that?" asked Brianna. She pointed over to one side, where a deep chasm separated the dreamy scene from a darker, foreboding landscape of sharp, jagged mountains and black, leafless trees. The sky was a myriad of violent color—red, black, and purple—and was crowded with more of those strange lumpy objects and heavy dark clouds that looked like smoke oozing from the pointy peaks. A bridge stretched over the chasm. It looked like an old-fashioned footbridge on the near side, with vine-covered railings and stone steps. But halfway across, it changed to black, angular beams, like steel girders disappearing into a low-lying fog.

"That is Skot'os," Ruwach said. "The enemy's lair in Ahoratos."

Brianna shivered a little. "Is that where those nasty butterflies come from?" she asked. "The Maribuntas?"

"Ah, yes," Ruwach said with a deep chuckle. "Here they are known as *Ents*. You will find that in Ahoratos, things that seem innocent and familiar can be very dangerous—even deadly. I suppose it is the same in your world. Like little lies, for instance." Ruwach's hood turned in Brianna's direction—she knew he was referring to her. She instantly remembered the little lie she'd told Landon about the Maribuntas.

Brianna lowered her eyes. "I didn't mean anything," she murmured.

"That's the danger." Ruwach's voice was stern but kind. He gestured with his robed arm. "Come inside now."

The kids followed Ruwach through the glittering gate and into the castle. They gazed in awe at the huge hall, at the center of which was a long table loaded with food. Fruits, cheeses, bread, cupcakes, even large bowls of ice cream. The kids forgot their sadness and weariness as they sat down at the table and began eating everything they could.

Brianna helped herself to a muffin. Chocolate chip, her favorite. It seemed like all her favorite foods were on the table. "I wish Levi was here," she said.

"Me too." It was a deep voice. But this was not Ruwach's voice, although it sounded familiar. They turned to look, shocked. There, standing with them in the castle, was someone they never expected to see.

"Mr. J. Ar?" Brianna gasped, rising to her feet. "Mr. J. Ar!" She ran to him, throwing herself in his arms. She didn't even seem to notice that he, too, was wearing armor.

The rest did. They stood motionless, thrilled but confused to see him without his trademark baseball cap and jersey.

"James is also a Prince Warrior," Ruwach said, noticing the disbelief on their faces. "Just as you are."

There was a short pause, the quiet filled with unspoken questions.

"How did you get here?" Evan asked finally, his mouth still stuffed with food.

"I saw Levi's drawing, so I figured he was probably going to end up here," said Mr. J. Ar, his arm still around Brianna. "I came—because I thought he might have some trouble."

Brianna's smile melted. "He's trapped," she said, sniffing.

"I know." Mr. J. Ar released her and walked to the table, sitting down heavily in a chair. "The same thing happened to me the first time I came here."

"Really?" Evan said.

"Went my own way, down my own path. Got in a mess of trouble. Lured across the bridge to Skot'os, then captured by the Forgers."

"Forgers?" Xavier asked.

"Yes, servants of the enemy."

"What saved you?"

"This." Mr. J. Ar rapped on his armor, which was more elaborate than the kids' single plates. His armor had several sections and covered his whole middle as well as his shoulders. He noticed their interest. "It grows with you, the more you use it," he explained. "But if you don't use it, it weakens and withers."

"Looks like you used it a lot," Evan said, admiration in his voice.

"I still do," said Mr. J. Ar. "There were some tough times. But I'm free now, thanks to the wisdom of Ruwach and The Book."

"Why didn't you tell Levi?" Brianna said. "Why didn't you warn him?"

"I did." Mr. J. Ar looked down at his hands thoughtfully. "Well, I've tried to, many times. But he may not have clearly understood. It's important to discover some things for yourself. Right, Ruwach?"

"That is right, James," said the little guide.

Mr. J. Ar let out a great, sad, sigh. Then he looked up, new energy in his voice. "Hope you've all eaten your fill, because we have work to do."

They all turned to Ruwach, who produced an object from his sleeve and set it on the table before them.

"A snow globe?" Brianna said, staring at it. It did look like a snow globe, except there was no snow in it. They all gathered around to look more closely.

There in the globe was a holographic image of their friend Levi, stuck up to his waist in something like gray cement. He was calling for help. His hand was locked in the grip of some sort of mechanical creature. Levi's arm had turned completely gray, the same color as the metal creature that held him captive. On the surface of the snow globe, letters flicked on and off:

L-E-V-I

Then the letters began to shiver, like they were being shaken. The kids held their breath, staring intently as the letters moved, rearranging, forming a new word:

E-V-I-L

Brianna raised a hand over her mouth to cover her gasp. The words *LEVI* and *EVIL* blinked back and forth, over and over.

"What does that mean? Is Levi turning evil?" Brianna asked.

"No, but he is in the grip of evil," Ruwach said.

Brianna straightened, a new fire gleaming in her eyes. She turned to Ruwach and Mr. J. Ar. "We have to go and get him out. Now!"

"We will," said Mr. J. Ar. His face was drawn with worry, but he managed a smile at Brianna's resolute tone.

"How can we get there?" Xavier asked. "To that place, where Levi is trapped."

"I have a friend who can take you," said Ruwach. He led the kids and Mr. J. Ar out to the wide courtyard and back down the glowing staircase to the shore. He stood before the water and raised his long, robed arms high in the air.

"Tannyn!" he shouted in a voice that reverberated off the glassy surface of the water. "Tannyn! Come!"

The water began to vibrate as if excited by Ruwach's command. A low rumbling sound emanated from below the surface. Evan stepped closer to Mr. J. Ar. Brianna moved closer to Xavier.

"What's happening?" she whispered.

The water shook ferociously until something broke through—something huge and silvery—something with *wings*.

Evan was sure it was the Loch Ness monster, although he'd never say it out loud with Xavier there. He stood still, trying not to cry out in fright.

The creature was enormous. Its wingspan seemed to reach to the edges of the lake itself. Water cascaded down its iridescent scales, and its long neck shook violently. Its head was surprisingly small with large yellow eyes. It opened its mouth, releasing a torrent of water and revealing long, spiky teeth. And then, weirdly, it seemed to smile.

"Don't be afraid," said Ruwach gently. "Tannyn will not harm you."

The giant creature settled onto the surface of the lake, blinking at them calmly.

"Gorp," it said. The kids looked at each other—Brianna grinned. There was something sort of comical about the creature, despite its fearsome appearance.

"Tannyn was once a slave," Ruwach said. "Forced to use his fire breath in the service of the ruler of Skot'os."

"So—it's not—dangerous?" Evan asked shakily.

"Tannyn wouldn't hurt a fly," Mr. J. Ar said. "Although he might deep-fry any Ents that happen to show up."

The creature waddled to shore, folding its wings and lowering its head submissively to Ruwach, like a big dog.

"Gorp," it said again. Brianna giggled. Xavier and Evan managed to smile.

"Tannyn will take you to Levi," Ruwach said.

"You want us to ride a *dragon*?" Brianna asked.

"He seems friendly," said Xavier, cautiously.

"He is not actually a dragon," said Ruwach. "More of a sea monster. With wings."

"Well, that explains *that*," said Evan.

"Tannyn's helped me out many times," Mr. J. Ar said. "He's the one that brought me out of Skot'os." He went up to stroke the giant creature's neck. It stretched its massive head around and gave him a gentle nudge.

"Gorp."

"Hello to you too," said Mr. J. Ar, smiling despite his lingering anxiety. "Long time no see." He glanced at the kids, who were still hanging back as Tannyn's head swung this way and that, its tongue lolling, smoke curling around its huge nostrils. "Hey, you can't always judge a book by its cover, right? So—who wants to go first?"

"I will," said Xavier, stepping forward. Tannyn lowered his head to the ground so Xavier could climb up his spiky neck to his back. Evan followed excitedly. Mr. J. Ar helped Brianna climb up too. There was enough space between the spikes on Tannyn's back for each kid to sit, holding onto the spike for balance. His skin felt slimy and scaly. The kids squirmed around, trying to get comfortable.

"Cake," Xavier said, looking back at Evan.

"Yeah, cake," Evan replied, cracking a smile.

"Wish my sisters could see this," Brianna said with a sigh. Mr. J. Ar climbed up, taking the spot in front of her.

"Farewell, warriors," said Ruwach, raising an arm. "James—take care." Mr. J. Ar nodded to him with a grim smile.

"Who's driving?" Evan asked, too preoccupied with the dragon-thing to notice their exchange.

"How do we steer?" echoed Brianna.

"Tannyn knows where to go," Mr. J. Ar said. "The enemy's ways are anything but original. He's been trapping people the same way since the beginning of time. Just hang on tight. Might get bumpy. Tannyn isn't the smoothest ride in Ahoratos."

He was right about that. Tannyn bolted straight off the ground like a streak of light. They held on for dear life.

"Keep your seat backs in an upright and locked position!" Mr. J. Ar shouted.

"Need—seat—belts!" Brianna shrieked.

Tannyn dipped and swooped crazily, as if struggling to get airborne.

"Does this thing even *know* how to fly?" Brianna yelled.

"Give him time," Mr. J Ar called back. "He needs to get his flying wings working. Spends most of his time underwater."

They thought for sure they would crash at least twice before Tannyn managed to level out.

"Stellar!" Brianna shouted as they soared—*really soared*—over mountain ranges, foothills, valleys, forests, and rivers. Always, the dark land of Skot'os seemed just over the horizon, never quite out of sight. Tannyn swerved this way and that to avoid the huge lumpy objects that floated in the golden sky.

"What are those things?" Brianna asked as they flew.

"Skypods," Mr. J. Ar shouted in answer. "We definitely don't want to disturb them."

Tannyn's great wings beat faster, taking them higher and higher, dipping and swooping around more skypods and mountain peaks. The kids shrieked in delight, as if they were on a breathtaking roller coaster ride. But their delight turned to screams when Tannyn suddenly folded his wings and dove, headed straight for the ground below.

"Hang on!" yelled Mr. J. Ar. "Landings aren't his specialty!"

Tannyn hit something solid and bounced three times before coming to a stop, lowering his head and opening his mouth. "Gorp."

The kids took a moment to catch their breath. Mr. J. Ar raced down the dragon's neck to the ground.

But there was no ground. When Xavier looked over the side of the creature's massive body, he saw that Mr. J. Ar seemed to be standing in the middle of the sky.

"Where are we?" he asked.

Mr. J. Ar crouched down to put his hands on the invisible surface on which they had landed.

"It's a dome," he said. "Like the snow globe Ruwach showed us."

Mr. J. Ar peered anxiously into the scene below. At first he saw nothing but a pulsing gray mass, like a heavy raincloud. He pounded on the barrier and the cloud broke apart—Ents. Hundreds of them filling the dome. They scattered as he pounded again, giving him a clear view of the scene below.

"Levi!"

CHAPTER FIFTEEN

Into the Dome

"Son! Hang on! I'm coming!"

From far above the surface of the dome, Mr. J. Ar saw his son stuck up to his waist in the ground, like he had sunk into concrete. His arm was held in the grip of a large metal figure, and the metal had spread halfway up Levi's arm. Levi was struggling to free himself, but he seemed very weak, as if he had lost not only the strength but also the will to fight.

Mr. J. Ar pounded on the dome and shouted again, but Levi couldn't hear him.

The other kids slid from Tannyn's back onto the invisible surface and knelt down beside Mr. J. Ar.

"Levi!" Brianna cried, shocked to see Levi in so much trouble.

"I've gotta get down there right now!" Mr. J. Ar stood up and went over to Tannyn, whispering fervently into the creature's small ear.

"This surface is solid. How are you going—?" Evan began. Before he could finish his sentence, the huge sea monster opened its mouth and breathed out a stream of blue fire that poured out onto the dome, making a noise like a gigantic blowtorch. The invisible glasslike surface melted away bit by bit, creating a ragged hole, seared black at the edges. The kids raised their arms to shield their faces from the raging heat. Mr. J. Ar spoke to Tannyn again, and it closed its mouth, stopping the fire, smoke still blowing from its nostrils.

"Levi!" Mr. J. Ar called down to his son through the new hole Tannyn had created. His voice echoed several times. "Can you hear me, son? I'm coming to get you! Just hang on!"

Levi looked up, and Mr. J. Ar could see the fear and desperation on his face. Levi tried to speak, but his voice was too weak to carry even on the echoes.

"If Tannyn makes the hole bigger, maybe he could fit through and take us down there," said Xavier.

"Can't do that," Mr. J. Ar said. "The dome might shatter and hurt him. Everyone give me your belts!" Mr. J. Ar's voice was harsh and flat, so unlike his usual deep, humored rumble. The kids hurried into action, removing their belts and handing them to him.

"What are you going to do?" Brianna asked. But Mr. J. Ar didn't answer. He touched the belts end to end and they fused together, creating one long belt. Mr. J. Ar put one end into Tannyn's mouth. Tannyn clamped down on it, holding it fast, as if he already knew what Mr. J. Ar wanted him to do. Mr. J. Ar quickly wrapped the other end of the belt around his own waist.

"What are you—" Xavier began. Mr. J. Ar drew his sword and held it aloft. The long, shiny blade gleamed in the sunlight.

"Whoa!" Evan gasped at the sight of the sword, secretly longing for his own.

Without another word, Mr. J. Ar jumped into the dome, still holding the sword in the air. The belt stretched like a bungee cord as he descended. The three kids watched, breathless, as Mr. J. Ar hit the ground hard, bouncing once, then twice, then finding his footing.

The Ents tried to dive for him with their evil stingers, but they couldn't seem to get near enough to do it. A mysterious power seemed to be emanating from the sword, holding them at bay.

"It's like a force field!" said Evan, even more admiring of the beautiful sword now.

Mr. J. Ar undid the belt and charged toward his son's captor, holding the sword in two hands. Sweat beaded on his brow, and a warriorlike cry rang out from his mouth. He slashed with the sword at the Forger's head, slicing it completely off in a single blow. The head bounced and rolled on the ground, the red eyes flickering like an overloaded circuit. Sparks flew from the tangled wires that stuck out from the Forger's metal neck like spindly tree roots. The kids, watching from above, were awestruck.

The headless Forger's metal arm still clung to Levi, refusing to let go. Levi squirmed, trying to free his arm, crying out softly. Mr. J. Ar slashed at the arm that held his son, striking it again and again, making sparks shoot off in all directions. But the arm still wouldn't let go. The Forger's other arm swung toward Mr. J. Ar, its hand opening like it wanted to trap him as it had trapped Levi. Mr. J. Ar dodged the arm, dropping the tip of his sword to the ground. As soon as he did the Ents began shooting their darts at him. He swung the sword back into the air to fend them off. Levi was calling to his dad, near tears. "It's no use, it's no use . . ."

Xavier turned toward the others. "It's not working. He can't do it alone."

"We need to help him," said Brianna. "Let's go!"

Before Xavier could even ask how they would do that, Brianna had grabbed the belt in both hands, wrapping her legs around it as well.

"Wait!" Xavier said. But she didn't. She'd already begun lowering herself into the dome, one hand under the other, working her legs expertly, like she'd done this a hundred times before. When she got near enough to the ground she jumped off and lunged toward Mr. J. Ar. She grabbed the mechanical arm of the Forger and pulled on it with her whole body, as Mr. J. Ar continued to strike it with his sword.

"Let go!" she yelled.

"We should get down there too," said Evan, watching from above. Xavier nodded. He grabbed the belt and began lowering himself down. Once he was on the ground, he held the belt steady for Evan to climb down as well.

They rushed over to help Mr. J. Ar. His attack had slowed slightly; he was wearing down under the strain of the heavy sword. Above them the Ents circled like hungry vultures, ready to dive in as soon as the sword dipped to the ground.

"Hold it up!" Xavier said, grabbing Mr. J. Ar's sword arm and lifting it into the air so the blade caught the sun. The Ents shrieked and backed off again.

"It's no use," Levi said, his head dropping to his chest.

"I—can't—do—it," Mr. J. Ar said, gasping for breath. "There's no way—"

"There is a way!" said Brianna defiantly. She turned to the Forger, balling her fists. "I said, 'Let go of my friend!'" She kicked the Forger's leg with her boot.

And something happened.

All of them stopped what they were doing and stared as a crack began to snake up the Forger's iron leg, widening as it went.

Brianna looked down at her feet. The boots looked the same—they hadn't sprouted any spikes. Yet they'd actually made a crack in the Forger's solid metal leg.

"Do it again!" said Xavier.

Brianna kicked again. Another crack appeared. The Forger's free arm swung toward her.

"Watch out!" said Xavier, reaching to grab Brianna out of the way. But then Mr. J. Ar hacked at the swinging arm with his sword, and it ruptured into a dozen pieces that scattered like shrapnel all around them.

"Keep going!" Mr. J. Ar yelled. Brianna, Evan, and Xavier kicked with all their might, making new cracks all over the Forger's metal body. Mr. J. Ar's sword blows were more effective now, smashing the Forger piece by piece. The Ents, disturbed by the Forger's destruction, flew up to the invisible barrier and stayed there, trembling.

Finally, with a horrendous creaky groan, like an engine bursting, the Forger's metal parts disintegrated into a shower of tiny fragments that fell to the ground. A sudden wind swept down from above, stirring up the fragments, gathering them, and spinning them up into a small tornado. The kids watched as the whirlwind of iron shards gathered speed until it shot upward, out of the dome. The Ents followed, shrieking and wailing in terror.

The warriors gazed up in wonder at the sight. For a long time no one could speak. It was Evan who finally broke the silence: "We did it." There was no elation in his voice, just relief and gratitude.

Mr. J. Ar looked at him and smiled, breathing raggedly. "You did. All of you." He seemed too overcome with emotion to say much more. Then he turned to Levi, knelt down, and reached for his son, who was still caught in the concrete-like ground. He put his arm around him slowly.

"You okay, son?"

Levi nodded silently and nestled his head into the crook of his father's arm as best he could. But then, the ground that held him began to crack just as the Forger had done. Levi felt himself loosening, the pressure from the solid surface giving way.

"I'm falling!" he cried.

Mr. J. Ar dropped his sword and put both arms around Levi as he was pulled down.

"Help him!" Xavier said, diving in to hold onto Mr. J. Ar so he wouldn't lose his balance. Evan grabbed Xavier around the waist and Brianna grabbed Evan, all of them pulling backward until they landed in a heap on the solid ground. They scrambled backward as the hole continued to widen, the ground melting away.

"Let's get out of here!" cried Brianna.

The cracks in the ground slithered to the edges of the invisible dome, then up to the surface. The entire dome was soon covered in a lacy pattern of cracks like a huge spiderweb.

"It's going to break!" Evan shouted.

Mr. J. Ar grabbed his sword and lifted it high in the air as chunks of the dome fell all around the kids, turning to dust as they did. Above them, Tannyn let out a muffled bellow as the dome gave way under his weight. He spread his wings and dove down, landing in a heap beside Mr. J. Ar. He opened his mouth, dropping the end of the belt, giving Mr. J. Ar a toothy grin.

"Gorp!"

"Hop on! Xavier, grab the belt!" Mr. J. Ar commanded, keeping the sword high. The kids scrambled up Tannyn's neck and nestled in between the spikes on his back. Mr. J. Ar followed, grabbing a spike to steady himself.

"Up, Tannyn!" he shouted. "Keep your heads down, kids!"

The kids obeyed, ducking their heads and closing their eyes as Tannyn spread his mighty wings and shot straight into the air. Brianna screamed, the sound lost in the deafening roar as Tannyn burst out of the enormous cloud of dust created by the collapsing dome. Tannyn opened his mouth and breathed a stream of fire, clearing a path through the mounting debris. When finally he emerged from the cloud into the clear sky, he let out a bellow of triumph. "Gorp!"

Mr. J. Ar opened his eyes and, taking a long, relieved breath, sheathed his sword. Tannyn leveled out, gliding more gently through the golden sky.

"It's okay, kids, you can look now," said Mr. J. Ar.

The kids opened their eyes cautiously and gasped at the magnificent view spread before them, their terror almost forgotten in the sheer thrill of the ride.

"Is this really a dragon?" said Levi, his arms wrapped tightly around a spike on Tannyn's back.

"Kinda," said Brianna. "Isn't he adorable?"

A few short minutes later, Tannyn swooped into the courtyard of the castle and bumped to a landing, nearly knocking all the kids off his back. Mr. J. Ar laughed, patting Tannyn's neck.

"Good dragon," he said.

"Gorp."

Tannyn lowered his head so his passengers could step down his neck to the ground. Mr. J. Ar went first, helping each kid in turn. Levi was last, falling into his dad's arms with a deep sigh.

"Thank you, Tannyn!" Brianna ran to the dragon and hugged him. Tannyn bobbed his head, his small eyes widening with something like happiness. Evan and Xavier called out their thanks as well.

"Gorp!" He let out a little burst of fire from his mouth and zoomed into the air, his wings spread wide for a split second before folding again as he dove for the lake, disappearing in another awesome splash.

CHAPTER SIXTEEN

The Evil Prince

Welcome back, Warriors." Ruwach came through the glittering gate to greet them. Xavier, Evan, and Brianna ran to meet him, along with Mr. J. Ar. Levi stayed on the ground staring up at the castle in utter disbelief. He was barefoot, and one of his arms was still metal all the way up to the shoulder. When he saw Ruwach, he put his head down in shame.

"We are glad to see you, Prince Levi," Ruwach said, coming nearer to him. The other kids watched silently.

"I'm not a prince," Levi said. "I don't deserve to be."

"Son," Mr. J. Ar said, kneeling down beside him, "Ruwach doesn't make mistakes. He called you Prince. Just as he called me, a long time ago."

Levi noticed for the first time that his father was wearing armor. "You?"

"And I messed up worse than you did, believe me. Most people do. But that's the wonderful thing about being a Prince Warrior of Ahoratos. Even when you mess up, you can be forgiven."

"But look at my arm," Levi said forlornly, lifting his heavy metal arm. "And my boots. I lost them."

His head was hung down so he didn't see Ruwach move closer to him holding a pair of boots, exactly the same as the ones Levi had left behind. Ruwach set them before Levi. "You mean these?"

"My boots—how did you find them?" Levi gasped.

"They were never lost. You just lost sight of them," Ruwach said.

"I won't do that again!" Levi said. He reached for the boots, but his hard gray fingers couldn't grasp them.

"Let me help you," Ruwach said. For the first time Levi saw a hand emerge from the guide's draped sleeve—at least he *thought* it was a hand, although it glowed silvery white, the fingers very bright and smooth. The glowing hand touched Levi's metal fingers. He felt a shiver, like a bolt of electricity, pass through his body. He shuddered but didn't pull his hand away. The metal on his arm felt warm, like it was heating up. It began to glow red and then slowly dissolved—first to a slippery, wet metallic coating, and then to a fine dust that fell away, revealing his own brown skin. All the kids watched in wonder as the pile of metallic dust was carried off by the wind.

Levi turned his arm this way and that, flexing his fingers.

"Thank you," he said. He touched each one of his fingertips. But there remained a small metal knob on the tip of one finger, where the Ent had bit him.

"As a reminder," Ruwach said, withdrawing his arm.

Mr. J. Ar bent down to Levi and pulled up his own sleeve. A rusted metal knot about the size of a dime sat a few inches above his elbow. Levi had never seen this scar before. He felt tears spring to his eyes and blinked them away, hoping the others couldn't see. Mr. J. Ar didn't say anything, just enfolded his son in a big bear hug.

"I want one too!" Brianna said. She ran up to hug Levi as well.

"Watch out for her," Evan said to Xavier, backing away. "She's a hugger."

Xavier smiled slightly.

"Now, put on your boots," said Mr. J. Ar. "And don't take them off."

Levi put on his boots and stood up unsteadily. The other kids grinned happily.

"Thanks, all of you, for coming to get me," Levi said. "You were really—brave."

"Ah, it was nothing," said Evan. "Cake."

"Yeah, cake," said Xavier.

"Speaking of cake . . ." Evan said, glancing at Ruwach. "Is there—?"

Ruwach's hooded head nodded. "And ice cream too," he said, a trace of humor in his usually stern voice. "Better get in there before it melts."

He spread his arms, and the great gate swung open. The four kids raced into the hall, where the long table still stood loaded with food—it looked as though nothing had yet been eaten.

Levi sat down to a huge bowl of ice cream and ate until he felt sick. It was the best feeling he ever had.

———

"Um, can I ask a question?" Xavier said once they had eaten their fill. "The black trees and sinkholes and the sand grobel and the Ents—why are they here? I mean, why does the Source allow them to exist? Can't he just make them disappear? Can't he destroy Skot'os altogether?"

Ruwach was silent a moment. All the kids watched him. It was always difficult to tell what Ruwach was actually looking at.

"Once," he said finally, in a softer, more mellow voice than usual, "there was harmony in Ahoratos. A great prince named Ponéros had dominion over the kingdom. But he was not content with it. He wanted more. He wanted to usurp the High Throne, which belonged to the Source. He rallied many of the creatures in Ahoratos to his side—by telling them they would have more freedom and power if he were their ruler. Many chose to believe him.

"Ponéros gathered his forces and rebelled against the Source. There was a terrible war, and Ponéros lost. But instead of destroying him completely, the Source revealed his infinite justice, righteousness, mercy, and love by merely banishing him to the other side of the chasm. There Ponéros must stay until the time of the Return, the time when the Source reveals himself to the whole world. Then there will be a great upheaval, and all those who have chosen Skot'os will be destroyed. Ponéros knows his time is short.

"But he still hasn't given up his quest. He's recruited many to his cause. He has taken many prisoners, ruined many lives. The Forger that you encountered, Levi—he was one of Ponéros's army. There are many more of them than can be counted, and they can take many forms."

"Yeah, I know," Levi said under his breath. "It looked just like me at first."

Brianna stared at him. "No—it was a metal monster thing. We all saw it."

Levi shook his head. "When I first saw it . . . *him* . . . he was a kid. And he looked exactly like me. Like a clone of me. He had a skateboard! He was wearing my T-shirt. His face and hands, everything was exactly like me. I thought maybe I was imagining things. But then he *talked* to me, in a voice that was just like mine. Told me he would help me. He got me to—take his hand." The last words were spoken almost in a whisper.

The others stood with their mouths agape, unsure of how to respond.

Ruwach's hood nodded. "The Forgers, like their master, are, above all, great deceivers. That is why you must always follow the Way of the Armor, because sometimes your worst enemy . . . is yourself." The message was clear.

Levi couldn't see Ruwach's eyes, but he could feel them turn to him. He nodded slowly.

"Got that right," he said.

"But what does this Ponéros guy want now?" Xavier asked. "He knows he can never rule Ahoratos, doesn't he? He's already been defeated."

"Yes, you are right, and he knows that too well. His only hope is to turn the whole world against the Source. And those like you—who have chosen the Way of the Armor—he wants to trick and deceive out of experiencing the joy of the victory the Source has already won. That is why more warriors are needed to rally against him and his quest. For every victory won here, there is one experienced there—on earth."

"But what can we do?" Brianna asked. "I mean, we're just kids."

"It begins with you," Ruwach said. He folded his arms into his robes, so that he suddenly looked very small again. "You must return now. Do not be afraid. Remember, you have everything you need."

Ruwach turned, the shining white doors opening to let him pass.

"But will we get to come back?" Brianna called after him.

"And will we get swords?" Evan added.

"What about unicorns?" Brianna asked.

Ruwach didn't answer. The gate closed behind him. They all stared at it for a few moments, not knowing exactly what to do next. Brianna was the first to turn around.

"Look!" Brianna said. The table of food was gone.

"Where'd it go?"

The kids huddled together, Mr. J. Ar with them. The walls seemed to be fading away, melting into the clouds beyond, so that soon they could see only clouds and light in all directions. The clouds wrapped around them, turning everything white and formless. The whiteness became unbearably bright—as if they were looking into the sun itself.

"Close your eyes," Mr. J. Ar said.

So, they did.

CHAPTER SEVENTEEN

Back to the Beginning

Levi sat up and looked around, blinking. He was sitting on the bench outside the Rec building, watching the skateboarders. His sketchbook was in his hand. He looked up at the sky. An after-dinner sky. It looked familiar. Was he—?

"Hey." Brianna sat down next to him.

He glanced at her but didn't speak. He looked down at his hands, his arms. They looked normal. They felt normal. He held up his fingers, and one of them had something on the tip. He touched it—it was hard, like metal.

"So that . . . really happened," he said.

"Yeah." Brianna was swinging her legs and looking listlessly into the distance.

"But how can it be, if we're—back before we left?" As far as he could tell, the scene in front of him was a repeat of the events earlier that day.

"I don't know. Time went backward, I guess," Brianna said with a shrug. "It happens."

"It does?"

She looked at him. "Why not?" She smiled. "You okay?"

"Yeah, I guess so." He put his head back against the wall. "I really messed up."

Brianna thought for a moment about how to respond. Her best friend had made a mistake, but he already knew that. She didn't need to rub it in. "So did I," she said after a few seconds. "Led Evan right into a Maribunta attack. Without the armor, we probably would have been goners."

"But you—you figured out how to break the Forger's hold on me."

"Yeah, how about that?" said Brianna with a grin. "So we mess up sometimes, but we get another chance. And maybe, we shine a little."

Levi shook his head. "Not me. I'm done."

"What do you mean?"

"There's no way Ruwach would trust me with another mission."

"Levi, you know that isn't true. He even said so. So did your dad." She paused. "Can you even believe your dad is a Prince Warrior?"

"Yeah, my dad's cool, I guess."

They were silent a moment, watching the skateboarders.

"So—what do we do now?" Levi said finally.

"I think it's time for you to go out there and skate," Brianna said. "And I go in to decorate. Right?"

"Yeah, I guess so. But I don't really feel like skating right now."

"Too tired?"

"No. But I kind of have a stomachache."

"Well, you *did* eat a lot of ice cream."

They were interrupted by a commotion from inside—raucous laughter and shouting. The skateboarders stopped riding and looked around. Some jumped off their boards to see what was going on.

"That would be Landon and his buddies," Brianna said, a keen sense of déjà vu settling in. "This is pretty weird, huh?"

"Yeah," Levi said. "Guess we need to go in now."

"Yep."

The skateboarders were already running to the building. Levi and Brianna got up and followed them.

It was the same sight as the last time—maybe this was *actually* the first time. Were they getting a second chance? Levi wasn't sure. He only knew that something had to be different.

Landon was taunting Manuel as the other kids laughed and pointed.

"Do you miss your mummy?"

The college student Mary Stanton emerged from the office, latte in one hand, cell phone in the other. "What's going on here? What are you kids doing?"

Brianna tugged on Levi's arm. "What are we supposed to do?"

Levi thought about the instruction he'd gotten in Ahoratos: *Wide is the gate that leads to destruction.* He knew what it meant now: *The right way is not always the easy way.*

All the kids were laughing. Jeff grabbed his elbow and whispered, "Get a load of that, huh?"

Levi glanced at his friends, the boys he hung out with every day. They all made fun of Manuel, with his goofy red glasses and enormous satchel that he carried around. He wore old-fashioned shoes and pants that never quite made it all the way to his ankles. Levi didn't know why Manuel came to the Rec at all—he never did any sports or games. Levi had always laughed right along with the other kids.

But looking now at the kid wrapped in toilet paper struggling on the floor, he remembered how it felt—to be stuck, unable to move, helpless, while all around him those awful Ents watched him, probably laughing, if Ents actually laughed. He imagined what all these kids would do if they had seen him struggling. And then he wondered what Ruwach would say, if Ruwach could see him now, standing on the outside of the circle, doing nothing. Watching.

But Ruwach probably can see me, can't he?

Levi took a breath.

"Hey, man, where you going?" Mikey asked, as Levi pushed through the crowd of onlookers to the center of the room. He stood before Landon, breathing slow, hoping no one could see how he was shaking inside. The kids around him quieted, wondering what he was up to.

"Get out of the way, stupid," Landon said, moving forward to push him aside.

"No," said Levi. Landon stared at him, surprise and anger moving over his face. Levi turned to the other kids. "You really think this is funny?" He looked at his skateboard friends—they were watching him, brows furrowed, like they thought he had gone crazy. "What if you were that kid? Would you be laughing then?"

Silence. The kids stared at him, shocked. Miss Stanton looked shocked too. She opened her mouth but nothing came out.

I'm gonna get creamed, Levi thought.

Ruwach's words came back to him: *You have everything you need.*

I have everything I need, Levi repeated to himself. *I don't need to be bigger, or tougher, or smarter. I just need to do the right thing.*

He glanced up, hoping to see the Crest shining above Landon's head, as it had before. It wasn't there. But he thought he could feel Ruwach's presence around him, the glowing white hand that had warmed his arm and healed him. He stood a little straighter. He felt a wave of something like courage flow through him.

He turned toward Landon. "You want to pick on someone, Landon?" Levi said. "Pick on me."

A murmur swept through the crowd—no one moved. Except Brianna.

"Yeah," she said, stepping up next to Levi and folding her arms together defiantly. "Me too."

They stood before the bully, unflinching. Landon's eyebrows knit together in rage. He balled his fists like he was about to take both of them out. But before he could make a move, another one of the girls came forward and stood with Levi and Brianna. Her name was Ivy, Levi remembered. She was about his age though much smaller. But she stood straight at Brianna's side, her hands on her hips, like she was ready for a rumble too.

Seeing the two girls stand up to the bully made the other kids shift around uneasily. For a moment, everyone was silent. But then Mikey came to stand beside Levi, then Jeff and Logan too. One by one, more kids stepped forward, forming a circle of protection around Manuel, who was lying on the floor, peeking through the folds of toilet paper, stunned. Miss Stanton dropped her phone.

There was a long moment of silence.

Landon's eyes glanced around the room, flickering slightly, no longer quite so certain he was in control. He balled up his fists, his arms stiffening, like he was about to explode. The bullies behind him shifted nervously. Tension hung in the air like a thick fog.

Finally, Landon relaxed his fists, shaking his head. He let out a braying laugh and backed away, punching one of his friends lightly with the back of his hand.

"Come on, dudes," he said. "Let's bounce."

Landon turned slowly and strode out of the building. After a moment his three friends followed him.

Levi saw his dad standing in the doorway. The bullies had to walk right past him as they left. Mr. J. Ar's eyes glowered, but his lips pursed in a settled, proud smile. Levi took a breath, his first full one in several minutes, and looked at Brianna. She grinned and hugged him. He pulled away quickly, turning to the others, who started to laugh and high-five each other as they reveled in their long-overdue victory.

Miss Stanton rushed forward to help Manuel off the floor and unwrap him from the toilet paper. Manuel smiled shyly at Levi.

"Thanks," he murmured.

"No problem." Levi felt lighter suddenly, older. Like he'd just climbed a mountain. "I know what it's like to have friends help when you need it." He glanced at Brianna, who grinned at him.

"You want me to call your dad, Manuel?" Miss Stanton said, balling up the toilet paper.

"No, thank you. I'm fine." Manuel stood straight, adjusting his glasses, although they still looked crooked.

Mr. J. Ar walked up to them and put a hand on Levi's shoulder. Levi thought he saw a tear in his dad's eye. "You okay, kids?"

"Yeah," said Levi.

"Stellar," Brianna said.

CHAPTER EIGHTEEN

Waking Up

Evan sat up in bed suddenly.

Bright sunshine poured in from his window. It was morning. He glanced down at the floor, where his book and flashlight still lay. Everything looked the same as when he'd gone to sleep. Maybe none of it had really happened. It was just a dream. He sighed, disappointed. He swung his legs out of bed and felt a chill. His legs were cold. One of them a bit more than the other.

He looked down at his pajamas, the same old knight pajamas he wore every night, except for when Mom took them to wash. And that's when he noticed that one of his pant legs was torn.

He remembered that when he had fallen in the race through the trees, a big branch had toppled on him, and Xavier had torn his pant leg to get him out.

So had it really happened, after all?

He still wasn't completely sure. He got up and went to look out at the backyard. Everything looked pretty much normal. There was the pond, glistening in the morning sunshine. Evan wondered suddenly if Tannyn was sleeping in there. Tannyn—he smiled to himself. He didn't think he had to be afraid of the Loch Ness monster anymore.

But something *was* different. He stared out the window, trying to figure out what it was. His eyes flitted around the familiar backyard for a few moments.

Then he saw it. The tree. The giant oak tree with the tire swing. It was split right down the middle and all blackened, like it'd been . . . *struck by lightning.*

Evan stood still—the wonder of it all, the terror and the beauty and the adventure, coming back to him. And now, his torn pajamas. And the wrecked oak tree in the yard.

So—it wasn't a dream after all!

It was real. He'd been to Ahoratos. He really *was* a prince. A Prince *Warrior.*

He knelt down and pulled his play armor from under his bed. He sighed, disappointed. It hadn't changed into his new armor. Not yet anyway. Ruwach had said they would get to take their armor back with them, someday. So that meant they would go back to Ahoratos. Ruwach would come for them again. He was sure of it.

Xavier—he had to talk to him. He burst into his brother's room, but he wasn't there. Strange. Xavier usually slept in. Had he gone back to Ahoratos already? Evan felt a little knot of anger form in his belly at the thought. *Follow the paths of old, and you will find peace.* Evan relaxed as Ruwach's voice flitted in his mind. He knew he didn't need to be angry about stuff like that anymore.

He got dressed and raced down to the kitchen. He was relieved to see Xavier sitting at the kitchen island, halfway through a bowl of Cheerios. Xavier looked up when Evan came in but didn't smile. Mom was pouring herself a cup of coffee.

"There you are, sleepyhead," she said. "I was about to come up and wake you."

"What happened to the tree?" Evan asked. Things weren't adding up. Xavier didn't seem all that different—he was still ignoring him.

"Bad storm last night. Didn't you hear it?" Mom asked. "I'm afraid lightning struck that big old tree. So sad. I know you boys loved that tree. I called the tree service to have it removed."

Evan looked at Xavier. Finally, his older brother met his gaze. He smiled the tiniest little bit and nodded. An exchange their mother did not notice.

"Yeah," Evan said. "Must have been a bad storm." *Real bad.*

"I'm surprised it didn't wake you up," Mom said.

"Yeah, me too." Evan sat down to pour a bowl of Cheerios. "Hey, Mom, can we go to the Rec today?" he asked. "I mean, am I allowed?"

"Sure, baby," Mom said. "Xavier, you want to go too?"

"Yeah," said Xavier, nonchalantly. "Sure. Whatever." Xavier got up to put his cereal bowl in the sink. He glanced over at Evan, eating his cereal. Evan seemed so happy. But Xavier had felt funny ever since he'd woken up, bothered by something. He knew what it was.

The truth holds everything together.

The belt in Ahoratos had fit every situation. It always made things right, even when it didn't seem like anything would work. He began to see why it was called Truth. Only truth would hold him and his brother together. He knew that he needed to tell it. The truth.

He cleared his throat. "Mom?"

"Yes, honey?" Mom leaned against the counter, the coffee mug cradled in her hands.

"I have something to tell you. About yesterday."

"Oh?"

Xavier saw Evan looking at him with worried eyes—he obviously thought Xavier was going to tell Mom about Ahoratos. Xavier shook his head slightly, reassuring him.

"You know when Evan got in trouble for fighting? Well, it was sort of—my fault."

"Oh really?" Mom didn't look all that surprised.

"I sort of—*provoked* him. I was making fun of him for being afraid. I'm sorry."

Mom let out a big sigh. "I'm glad you told me. That was the right thing to do. Maybe you should stay home today. I have lots of chores you could do—"

"No!" Evan interrupted. "I mean, I don't care what he did. I think he was trying to help me in his weird way. But anyway, I don't want him to stay home. I'll help do the chores, if we can both go to the Rec. Okay, Mom?"

He smiled winningly at her. She looked at him with narrowed eyes.

"Who are you, and what have you done with Evan?"

He rolled his eyes. "Mom . . ."

"Okay, okay," Mom said, glancing quickly at Xavier. "I'll make you a list, and when it's done, you can go to the Rec."

"Cool!" Evan was grateful. Now he and Xavier would have time to talk about what happened without the danger of any parents or adults overhearing them.

"But don't forget, school starts next week and we still have some school shopping to do."

"All right," Evan said glumly. He was not looking forward to going to a new school and having to make friends all over again. He knew Xavier wasn't either. But at least they knew Levi and Brianna—that would help.

―――――

Xavier and Evan rode in the backseat of the van to the Rec. Mom had the radio on and was singing along with the music.

"I turned on the phone this morning when I got up," Xavier whispered to his brother. "And this was on it."

He showed it to Evan, whose eyes widened. "Did you download it?"

There was an app on the phone that hadn't been there before. The word *UNSEEN* stood out in capital letters underneath a familiar symbol.

"It's the Crest!" Evan said, keeping his voice low so his mom wouldn't hear. "Maybe Ruwach sent it. Awesome! What does it do?"

"I don't know. I'm afraid to open it."

"Maybe it'll take us back to Ahoratos!"

"What, an app?"

"Sure—try it!"

"We're in the car! If we disappeared right now Mom would freak out and probably drive into a tree. Let's wait until we get there."

Evan slumped back in the seat. "Okay."

CHAPTER NINETEEN

A Is for App

Evan saw Levi in the skateboard park and ran up to him.

"Hey!" he shouted excitedly. Levi spun around on his skateboard and looked at him with a blank expression. For a second Evan thought Levi didn't know who he was, and he was about to feel very dumb standing there, waving. But then Levi raised his hand in a small wave, and Evan let out a breath of relief. He watched as Levi skated toward him, spun around, and flipped his board into the air, catching it one-handed.

"Hey," Levi said. He bobbed his chin up slightly, his version of a greeting. Evan thought it was cool.

"Hey," Evan said. Xavier walked up as well, his hands in his pockets. He didn't say anything at first, just smiled awkwardly.

"What's up?" Levi said.

Xavier shrugged. "Not much. You?"

Levi shrugged. They looked from one to the other, not speaking, as if they already knew what the others were thinking. Then, as if on cue, all three broke into nervous laughter. The awkwardness they'd felt a moment ago dissolved.

Together they walked over to a picnic table and sat down. Levi leaned his board against the bench. Xavier pulled out his phone and showed Levi the app.

"That's weird," Levi said. "I have that on my phone too." He took his phone from his pocket to show them. "It just showed up yesterday. *UNSEEN*. I didn't know what that meant, but then I saw it also had the Crest."

"Did you open it?" Evan asked.

"Yeah. But it was just a lot of jumbled up images. I thought it was damaged. So I trashed it. But then when I looked at my phone this morning, it was back."

"Whoa," Evan said. "Kind of like your boots. Maybe it can't be lost." He turned toward Xavier. "Open it, Xavi."

Xavier unlocked his phone and opened the app. They all waited tensely for something to happen, as if they thought they might get sucked down into the phone. They saw nothing but a series of strange patterns and symbols, just as Levi had said, like a jigsaw puzzle with all the pieces mixed up. Xavier pressed the screen a few times, but the image didn't change.

"Weird," said Evan. "But you know, it sort of reminds me of The Book—you know, the scrambled words. Ruwach had to unscramble them to show us our instructions."

"Maybe only Ruwach can do it," said Xavier.

"So what do we do—call him? How do we even do that?"

"I think with Ruwach it's more like a 'Don't call me, I'll call you' sort of thing," said Xavier. They all laughed.

"Whatcha doing?" Brianna suddenly plopped down at the table next to Xavier. She was wearing her signature pink hoodie, and her lips sparkled with a fresh application of lip gloss. Her curly brown hair was pulled back into a thick ponytail. She smiled at Xavier, who smiled back. He shoved over into Evan to make room for her.

"Check this out," Xavier said, showing her his phone.

"Oh yeah!" Brianna said. She pulled her phone out of her pocket. "I thought I lost my phone when we—you know—but when I got back it was still in my pocket. Weird, huh? When I turned it on, that app was there. I never even downloaded it."

"Why do you think it's called *UNSEEN*?" said Levi.

"I guess cause that's what Ahoratos is—the unseen world. It's here, but we can't see it, unless we're there," said Brianna.

"Uh-huh," said Evan, nodding, although he still looked slightly confused.

"Did you open it?" Xavier asked Brianna.

"Yeah, but it didn't make any sense. So I just deleted it. But then it came back on its own!"

"Same here," Levi said. "We can't get past the first screen."

"Let's try doing it at the same time," Xavier said. "Maybe that would make it work."

They put all three phones together and tapped on the app. All three apps opened at once. But the result was the same—nothing but strange patterns and symbols.

Just then, Landon and his friends passed by, giving Levi a dirty look as he did. The kids hid their phones, in case Landon would get it in his head to steal them or break them or something.

"He's got it in for me now," Levi said.

"Something happen?" Xavier asked.

Levi told the brothers about the encounter with Landon, Brianna adding many colorful details.

"Whoa. So time went *backward* for you?" Xavier said. "And you got to do it again?"

"Yeah. Didn't that happen for you?"

Xavier shook his head. "Well, maybe it did. We were both asleep."

"Do you think we'll get to go back to Ahoratos?" Evan whispered.

"I hope so," Brianna said, secretly hoping their next visit wouldn't involve a sand grobel or evil Maribuntas.

"Hey, guys."

They looked up to see the dorky kid Manuel standing before them, smiling awkwardly. He was wearing an "Einstein Rocks" T-shirt and carrying a satchel. He pushed his glasses up his nose.

"Hey," Levi said. "Whassup?"

"Can I . . . talk to you? Just for a second. I don't mean to interrupt."

"It's okay," Levi said. He was kind of surprised. Manuel had never tried to talk to him before. Or, maybe he had, but Levi had been too busy with his own friends to pay any attention. Levi glanced over at his skateboarder friends, hoping they weren't looking. Then he moved over so Manuel could sit next to him.

"These are my friends, Be—*Brianna*, Xavier, and Evan."

"Nice to meet you," Manuel said, setting his satchel on his lap.

"Hey," they all answered in return.

"Thanks again, for yesterday," Manuel said to Levi and Brianna. "That was really—amazing. And nice. I mean, no one's ever done anything like that for me before . . ."

"Yeah, it's okay," said Levi, shifting around slightly.

"But I . . . well, I'm not quite sure how to ask this, but . . . there was something I saw when all that was going on that I wondered about. Here, let me show you." He opened his satchel and pulled out a large, dusty book.

"Hey, I have that book!" Evan said. The book had the Crest of Ahoratos on the cover.

"Me too," said Brianna. "How'd you get it?"

"My mother gave me this book," Manuel said, "before . . . anyway, she told me her father had given it to her, and his father had given it to him. She said it was a special book, but I never actually read it. It seemed too babyish for me, with the big type and pictures. I only read science books, usually." He paused, grinning slightly in embarrassment. "But when I saw this symbol on your shirt yesterday—"

"*My* shirt?" Levi said, surprised.

"Yes, it was on the back of your shirt, and hers too. I remembered it and so—"

"My shirt had a Tony Hawk design on it," Levi said.

Manuel's eyes, already large behind his thick glasses, got even larger. "Perhaps I was imagining it. I'm so sorry." He shoved the book back in his satchel and got up to leave.

"Wait," Xavier said. Levi and Evan glared at him. Xavier leaned in to talk to them in a softer voice. "He saw the Crest, same as us."

"But it wasn't on my shirt," Levi said.

"He still *saw* it. So he must know. I mean, maybe he's *meant* to know about it. He's got the book too. We should tell him."

"But he wasn't called," Levi said.

"Maybe that's our job," Xavier replied. Levi didn't respond.

Manuel was still standing by the picnic table, holding his satchel, looking at them awkwardly.

"Sit down, Manuel," Xavier said. "We need to—tell you something."

"Tell me what?" Manuel sat down eagerly, leaning in.

"What you saw," Xavier said slowly, searching for the right words, "was the Crest of Ahoratos."

"A . . . crest?"

"Ahoratos, from that book you have. It's a real place. And we've been there."

"Really?" Manuel's eyes got big as saucers. He pulled a notebook out of his satchel and began writing things down. The kids went on to tell him all that had happened in Ahoratos, about Ruwach, even about Tannyn. After a while Manuel stopped writing and just listened, trying to absorb all this information, not sure if he could really believe it or not.

"You're not—putting me on, are you?" he asked when they were done.

Evan wrinkled his nose. "Putting you on? Like a jacket or something?"

"It's an expression," Manuel said, blushing again. "My mom . . ." He didn't finish. There was an awkward silence.

"It's okay. My mom has weird expressions too," Evan said, trying to be kind.

"Sorry about your mom," Levi said.

Manuel shrugged.

"Maybe you should come with us," Levi said. "Next time we go. I mean, if you need proof—"

"*If* we go," Xavier said. "What if we don't get called again?"

"We still need to get our swords," Evan said. "And shields."

"And helmets," Levi said.

"But how can we get back there?" Brianna asked.

"Ruwach came to us when we were asleep," Evan said.

"I wasn't asleep," Levi said.

"Are you sure?"

"Sure I'm sure! We saw the crest over Landon's head and we grabbed it—"

"You grabbed it?" Manuel repeated.

"Bean and me."

"Bean?" Manuel's eyes narrowed, and he pushed his glasses up his nose.

Levi pointed at Brianna. She rolled her eyes.

"Perhaps I could create a computer model of the Crest," Manuel said. "Like a 3-D simulation. Then we could all—"

"Jump into the computer screen?" Xavier said, snickering. "Seriously?"

Manuel's face fell. "It was just an idea."

"Maybe if you made a hologram projection, like they do in that show *Jet Force*," Levi began. He knew about

Manuel's penchant for science projects. He figured if anyone could do it, Manuel could.

"I'd have to develop a program," Manuel said. "It would take time—"

Evan broke in. "Or you could just go over and try to get Landon to start bullying you again, then maybe the Crest will show up."

"Evan!" Brianna said, flicking him lightly with her finger in the back of his head. Her lips were pursed. Evan was stunned by all the glitter.

"What are you kids up to?"

They all jumped. Mr. J. Ar stood before them, arms folded over his barrel chest, his expression very stern. They all fell silent, not wanting to meet his eyes. Maybe they weren't supposed to talk about Ahoratos—maybe he was going to scold them. It sure looked like it.

Then Mr. J. Ar broke into a grin. "Gotcha."

Evan laughed. "You got us." They all breathed a sigh of relief.

"I figured you kids were trying to figure out how to get back to Ahoratos," Mr. J. Ar said.

"How'd you know?" Xavier asked.

"Because that's what my friends and I always used to do too," said Levi's father with a laugh. He leaned down over them, resting his fists on the table.

"Did you ever figure it out?" Brianna asked.

Mr. J. Ar shook his head. "Well, there *was* a way I learned. But I don't think I'll tell you. I'll let you figure that out on your own." He paused, chuckling. "Don't worry—you'll go back. In the meantime, anyone up for a game of b-ball?"

"I am!" Xavier said.

"Me too!" said Evan.

"Me three," Brianna said.

Levi looked at her. "Really? Won't it mess up your hair?"

Brianna's gaze narrowed. "You afraid I'll beat you?"

Evan snickered. Xavier elbowed him.

"I'm in," said Levi, although he gazed longingly at his skateboard.

Mr. J. Ar looked over at Manuel.

"Oh, I'm terrible at sports," said Manuel, waving his hands in the air. "No hand-eye coordination, apparently. Plus, I have asthma. And look!" He pointed to the sky, which was clouding over quickly. "I think it's going to rain soon anyway."

"That's weird. It was perfectly sunny a minute ago," Brianna said, looking up at the sky with a frown.

"It's not raining yet," Mr. J. Ar said. "We've got time for a game."

"I don't know . . ." said Manuel.

"Come on," Evan said with a laugh. "We'll go easy on you, promise."

Manuel stood near the basket while the other kids ran around the court dribbling and passing the ball. Every once in a while someone passed him the ball, and he threw it at the basket. He missed by a mile. But he didn't seem to mind. It was sort of fun. He couldn't remember the last time anyone had invited him to play a game.

He usually stayed in his room, by himself, working on his experiments and inventions. It was just easier than dealing with other kids, because they always thought he was too weird.

His dad made him go to the Rec. His dad taught summer courses at the local college and didn't like Manuel being all alone in the house, especially since he almost burned it down once in a science experiment gone wrong.

"It was just a *small* explosion," he had told his father when he came home. "I only singed the curtains a bit." His father had been less than understanding.

So now Manuel was doomed to spend the rest of his summer at the Rec, being tormented by bullies and otherwise ignored. He'd been counting the days until school started—five more to go! But now, all of a sudden, he had some friends. All because of that awful mummy incident.

"Yo, Manuel, you're up!" Xavier dribbled around Levi's flailing arms and passed the ball to Manuel. He caught it, the force of the ball nearly knocking the wind of out him. "Throw!"

Manuel saw Evan coming for him. He panicked, looked up, and threw the ball into the air underhanded. It went through the net—the wrong way, in the bottom and out the top.

Evan and Levi fell down laughing. Xavier caught the ball and gave Manuel a gentle knock on the shoulder. "You just need to practice, dude."

Manuel smiled—but his smile faded when he saw who had just come into view.

Landon sauntered across the court and sat down on the bench along the side. He was alone, no gang of bullies backing him up. Manuel had never seen him alone before. Landon's menacing eyes bored holes in Manuel's stomach.

"Hey, guys, I think I'm going to go in now," Manuel said. He was having a hard time breathing. "It's just my asthma. I need to get my inhaler." As if in answer to his dilemma, a drop of rain fell on his glasses. He wiped the lens and squinted, glancing up. Dark clouds were rolling across the sky, gobbling up the last bit of blue.

"Oh, look, it's raining anyway. We should go in. Shouldn't we?"

"It's not raining *that* hard," said Evan.

"Besides, you can't leave in the middle of a game!" said Levi.

"Well, I . . . I really don't think . . ." Manuel stuttered, backing away from the court. Levi followed his gaze and saw Landon sitting there on the sidelines, watching. He nodded, understanding.

"Don't worry, my dad is here. Landon's not going to try anything."

Xavier dribbled the ball a couple of times, but before he could shoot, Mr. J. Ar blew his whistle and put his hands out for the ball. Xavier bounced it to him. Manuel breathed a sigh of relief—perhaps they were going in after all. More fat raindrops were falling, making splotches on the court.

But then Mr. J. Ar turned to Landon. "Hey, Landon. You want to play?"

The four kids froze.

"What?" Manuel whispered, his knees actually knocking together.

"Come on," Mr. J. Ar continued, ignoring the trepidation he was causing in Manuel.

"Dad, we really don't want him in the game," Levi whispered hoarsely.

"If he plays, I'm not playing," Evan said. "He'll play dirty and probably kill us."

Landon stood up, as if to accept the invitation. The boys tensed. Then Landon waved them off, shook his head, and shuffled away.

Manuel's shoulders relaxed, and he breathed a little easier. Maybe he wouldn't need his inhaler after all. The danger seemed to have passed.

"Come *on*, let's play," shouted Evan.

A loud boom of thunder clapped overhead. All the kids jumped, startled.

Mr. J. Ar looked up. "Looks like a storm coming through," he said.

"I knew it," said Manuel eagerly. "We should really go inside. Deadly lightning strikes are 22 percent more common during outdoor sports activities . . ."

Heavy dark clouds were swiftly rolling in. Everything around them got dark very suddenly, like a giant shade had been pulled across the sky. Another loud crash of thunder. A gust of wind caught them unawares, snatching the ball from Mr. J. Ar's hands. It bounced over to Manuel, who managed to catch it before it got away. He held onto it tightly as another gust of wind nearly knocked him over.

Mr. J. Ar blew his whistle. "Everyone in!" he yelled as lightning streaked through the dark clouds above. Rain splattered onto the basketball court. With another huge crack of thunder the clouds seemed to split open, pouring down rain from a celestial bucket.

Mr. J. Ar trotted off the court, corralling the kids into the building. Xavier, Evan, Levi, Brianna, and Manuel followed quickly. The girls on the volleyball court and the kids playing kickball scurried into the building, covering their heads.

Once inside the Rec most of the kids went straight into the gym to resume their games. Others sat down at tables and started making lanyards and doing crafts. Miss Stanton scurried around passing out the art supplies, trying to get all the kids settled in some activity to keep them occupied. Levi, Xavier, Evan, and Brianna sat together at a table and pulled out their phones once more to try and figure out how to work the app.

Manuel opened his satchel and pulled out his inhaler, although he didn't really need it. He stood near the door, leaning against the wall, hoping to just stay out of everyone's way. The rain pounded hard on the roof, lashing the windows. He turned to look out the small window in the door and saw that Landon was still standing by the fence, not making any move to take shelter. He was just staring at the rain, getting drenched, oblivious to the lightning and thunder.

Manuel's gaze drifted to the rain pounding the basketball court. Cloudbursts were fairly common this time of year, but still—there was something very odd and unsettling about this particular storm. The puddles on the court were filling up very fast—nearly the entire basketball court was already underwater. That seemed highly unusual.

And then something even weirder happened. A giant gust of wind swooped into the basketball court and began churning the water. The puddle on the court was now spinning into a whirlpool, rising up into the air. Manuel's mouth dropped open in alarm. He motioned to his new friends to come over and look. Levi got up and went to stand by him.

"Do you see that?" Manuel said, pointing.

"Yeah," said Levi. "Some crazy rain."

"What's the matter?" Brianna had come over as well and was looking over Levi's shoulder.

The wind was so strong now it bent the trees around the court nearly double and blew the swings up and over the swing sets in full circles. The whirlpool in the basketball court grew taller, churning even faster—it looked now like a small tornado.

Xavier and Evan joined the others at the door. "What's going on?" said Xavier.

"It's bad," said Evan. "Like last night."

Xavier and Evan glanced at each other.

"Look!" shouted Brianna. "Are you all seeing what I'm seeing?"

Hovering in the air above the fast-growing tornado was a large golden image of the Crest of Ahoratos. It turned slowly, glimmering through the dark sky.

"Whoa!" said Evan.

What they could not see was Ruwach, in the midst of the whirlwind, twisting his robed arms in a circle as if making the winds go faster, picking up more and more of the rainwater and spinning into the air.

"Come, Warriors."

"Did you hear that?" Xavier said.

"Hear what?" said Brianna.

"Come, Warriors. Into the wind. Now!"

"I heard it, too, I think," said Evan. "It sounded a little like—*Ru.*"

"Ruwach," Xavier said. "And yeah, it did."

"Into the wind!"

They all heard it that time. The kids looked from each other to the tornado that whipped even higher. They didn't have to speak it aloud. They knew what they were supposed to do.

"Should we tell your dad?" Evan asked, glancing around the room. The kids were absorbed in their activities, ignoring them. A group of girls had put on some music and were dancing. Mr. J. Ar was by the office door, talking on his phone. He didn't seem to notice the kids standing at the door.

"I think he'll figure it out," said Levi.

"Let's go!" said Evan. He was the first to move, pressing open the door and charging into the rain. Xavier followed close behind, ducking his head against the wind.

"Come on!" said Brianna, pulling on Levi's arm. "Hurry! Before someone notices us!"

Levi turned to Manuel. "You too." He grabbed Manuel's sleeve and pulled him out after him.

Manuel tried to resist. "No . . . no . . . dangerous . . . my inhaler!"

Levi ignored his pleas as he followed Brianna out into the rain.

"Let's go!" Brianna said. "We're going back to Ahoratos!"

Mr. J. Ar heard the door slam shut and looked up. Frowning, he glanced around the room and noticed that the five kids, including his son, were no longer there. He went to the doorway and looked through the window, just in time to see them disappear into the whirlwind on the basketball court. Mr. J. Ar folded his arms and sighed, smiling to himself.

Landon, still standing out in the rain, saw them disappear too.

PART THREE

Once Freed, Always Free

CHAPTER TWENTY

Into the Wind

The kids spun crazily as the whirlwind lifted them off the ground, sweeping them toward the dark sky. The wind was so fierce it made their skin ripple and took their breath away. Xavier struggled to open his eyes to see where the others were—he saw Evan tumble past him and reached out to grab his arm.

"Stay together!" Xavier shouted over the keening whistle of the wind, although he felt his words being pushed back down his throat. Levi managed to get hold of Brianna, then he reached out to grab Evan's other arm. Brianna tried to get to Manuel as he pinwheeled by, but she couldn't get a grip on his flailing arms and legs.

"Hold still!" Brianna shouted at Manuel.

"We're gonna die!" wailed Manuel. He grabbed his glasses before they flew off his face, holding onto them like an anchor.

"Oh *please!*" Brianna cried in frustration.

One of Manuel's legs knocked against Xavier, and Xavier caught it before Manuel could whirl away again. Brianna grabbed the other leg, so they held Manuel upside down, but it was better than nothing.

"What's—hap—pen—ing?" cried Manuel. He let go of his glasses to wrap his arms around one of Xavier's legs as the kids continued to spin faster and higher.

"Not sure yet!" Xavier shouted back. "Just hang on!" They banded closer together, shutting their eyes, holding onto each other for dear life.

After what seemed like an eternity, the wind began to lessen, and the kids dropped downward, slowly at first, but then gaining speed.

"We're falling!" Manuel shrieked. "We're going to die!"

Within seconds they dropped out of the whirlwind and onto soft ground. And, just like that, the sun came out. The wind was gone. It was quiet, except for the distant sound of rushing water. The kids rolled to sitting positions, shaking their heads and gazing around them.

Manuel adjusted his glasses and stared, blinking, sure he was seeing things. He wasn't at the Rec anymore. He knew that for certain. He was nestled in soft grass at the edge of a steep chasm. Far below was a shallow, fast-moving stream, water rushing over rocks and large boulders. He looked up to see a bridge spanning the chasm. Only Manuel had never seen this kind of bridge before. It started on one side as a dreamy, cobbled bridge covered in vines and moss, with stairs leading up to the center. But right in the middle it morphed into black riveted girders, like an old railroad bridge. The other side of the chasm was draped in fog so dense that no details were visible. The sky was really odd too—it was a kind of golden color on one side, but dark red on the other. Both sides were dotted with large, lumpy gray objects that looked like floating rocks.

"Where are we?" Manuel whispered. "Canada?"

"Welcome to Ahoratos," said Levi, shaking off the dizziness in his head.

"This is *Ahoratos*?" Manuel blinked several times to make sure he wasn't imagining things. "What's over there?" He pointed to the other side of the chasm.

"I think that's Skot'os," said Xavier, standing up for a better view. "Although it looks different now than it did before."

"Skot'os?" Manuel said. He remembered that word from the book his mom had given him. There was something very unpleasant about it.

Brianna stood up, brushing grass off her clothes. "My hair," she said, corralling the loose strands of her hair back into a neat ponytail. Manuel gaped at her, unable to believe that she could be so concerned about her hair after such an ordeal.

"We're back," said Evan, jumping up excitedly. "Can you believe it? That was fast. Only where's the Water? We need to get to the Water!"

"Down there," said Xavier, pointing down to the stream below. They all looked—the Crest of Ahoratos shimmered on its surface. It was definitely the Water.

"How do we get down there?" Brianna said, frowning. "Seems a little steep to climb down. And we don't have our boots on."

"I think we'll have to jump," said Xavier.

"Jump?" Manuel paled. "*Jump?* It's like four hundred feet at least! We'll be killed, our bodies dashed on the rocks . . ."

"Oh man," said Evan, shaking his head.

Levi got up and looked over the edge. "I'm kinda with Manuel on this one."

Brianna made a disgusted noise. "What are you all so afraid of?" she said, tossing her ponytail. She marched to the edge of the chasm, straightening her shoulders. She looked down, feeling the blood drain from her face as she saw just how far down it was. But the Crest was there, floating on the Water. She had to show the boys she wasn't afraid, that she could do anything they could do. She raised her head and took a deep breath. "Like this."

She shut her eyes and jumped. Manuel cried out and looked away, unable to watch what happened. He heard—nothing. Not even a splash.

"She did it!" Levi said. Manuel opened his eyes and looked down into the chasm. Brianna was nowhere to be seen, but there was a faint tinge of red in the Water around the strange symbol.

"See the red color?" Xavier said. "I saw that when Evan went into the Water the first time. I think it means she made it to the Cave. She's safe."

"That's good," said Levi with a sigh of relief.

"There's a cave down there?" Manuel pushed up his glasses. "Must be deeper than it looks," he mused.

Levi laughed and went to the edge. He looked over once and shrugged. "Here goes nothing!" he said. And he jumped, doing a flip in the air before diving straight down. Manuel watched this time as Levi descended to the Water—but instead of being dashed on rocks he seemed to go straight through without even a splash. And there was that red tinge again, appearing briefly then vanishing.

"You good to go, Van?" Xavier asked his little brother.

"Sure, no problem," said Evan. He stood at the edge of the chasm, hesitated only briefly, then held his nose with one hand and stuck his other hand in the air, as if he were holding a sword. "Ahoratos!" he yelled, like a battle cry. Then he jumped and disappeared into the Water below, leaving only that tint of red. Manuel shook his head in disbelief. Then he saw that Xavier was looking at *him*. He backed away slowly, waving his hands in the air.

"No . . . no . . ."

"Come on," said Xavier. "I'll help you. Grab my hand."

Xavier went to the edge of the cliff and put out his hand for Manuel, who took a few tiny steps toward him.

One, two, three . . . Manuel counted the steps in his head. *Four, five, six* . . .

Manuel always counted when he found himself in terrifying situations. His mother had taught him that a long time ago. *If you're going through a bad time, start counting.* He wasn't sure why, but he always did it. Yesterday, in the mummy incident, he'd gotten to forty-three.

Seven, eight . . .

He reached out and took hold of Xavier's whole arm.

"When I count to three, we're going to jump, okay?" Xavier said, locking his arm around Manuel's so he wouldn't be able to let go.

Nine, ten . . .

Manuel nodded stiffly.

"One . . ."

"Wait!" Manuel said. He took off his glasses and shoved them in his pocket. "Okay."

Xavier nodded. "Two . . ."

He never said three. He jumped on two, taking Manuel with him over the edge.

Manuel let out a bloodcurdling wail as he dropped into the chasm, certain he was going to die once again. "Eleven, twelve!" He shouted these last two numbers out loud, knowing they would be the last words he would ever utter. *Not very memorable,* he thought bleakly.

Within seconds they hit the Water. Manuel thought his heart had stopped beating altogether. He felt a *whoosh*, like he was being flushed down a toilet (something he had never imagined actually doing), and then he waited for the end.

When he opened his eyes again, he was standing on solid ground. He didn't seem to be dead, nor was he even wet. He raised his arms and felt his face, his chest, his stomach. He looked down at his legs. Everything was intact and appeared to be working. He pulled his glasses out of his pants pocket, expecting them to be smashed to pieces. But there wasn't a single crack in them.

A luminous landscape appeared before him: blue mountains and icicles and snowflakes . . . *wait* . . . *no* . . . They weren't mountains or icicles. They were . . .

Xavier came into view, grinning.

"Welcome to the Cave," he said.

A cave?

If this was a cave, it was the strangest one Manuel had ever seen. The rock formations glowed as if lit from the inside. Little puffs of light floated on the air around him. And most amazing of all—he was completely dry. He was not even wearing his own clothes anymore. He glanced down at the thick gray shirt and pants—the Crest of Ahoratos glowed faintly on his chest. *When did I change?* he wondered. Perhaps he had been knocked out by the fall. *Or maybe,* he concluded, *this is all a dream.*

"You've brought a friend, I see," said a big, echoing voice. "Welcome, Prince Manuel."

Manuel couldn't tell if the voice was inside or outside his own head. He turned to see a tiny, purple-robed figure standing before him, his face concealed by a large hood. The other kids were gathered around him, dressed just as Manuel was.

"Uh, hello," Manuel said in a shaky voice, wondering why the voice in the hood had called him a prince.

"I've been waiting for you. Don't be afraid. I am Ruwach. I am your guide when you are in Ahoratos."

"Nice to . . . meet you . . . Ru-wach." Manuel bent forward in an awkward bow ('cause that's what princes do, right?). Evan stifled a laugh. "I'm glad to be here . . . I think." He tried to sound casual, so the others wouldn't think he was a complete chicken. It wasn't really fair, after all—obviously they'd been here before.

"You have to come to the Cave first," Evan said, stepping forward with great assurance, "to get your armor. And you always have to come through the Water. It's marked with the Crest—you know that symbol from the book—so you can't miss it. That's really important."

"Armor?" Manuel said.

"Yeah," Levi said. "You can't survive in Ahoratos without it."

"Is it . . . dangerous there?" asked Manuel.

"Sometimes," said Xavier.

"There are Forgers," Brianna said. "And sand grobels. And evil butterflies called Ents. And sometimes the ground turns to quicksand, and sometimes buildings fall down, and you really have to be prepared."

"Hey, guys, take it easy on him," Xavier said. Manuel's mouth had dropped open in alarm. "He just got here."

"You need to get your armor on," Evan said. "Right, Ru?"

"Don't call him that," whispered Xavier, giving him a little shove.

"You are right, Prince Evan. Come, Prince Manuel." Ruwach reached out one robed arm toward Manuel, letting him know he was being summoned. "Follow me." The guide turned and began moving toward one of the dark tunnels. Manuel felt compelled to follow.

"The rest of you need to get prepared as well." Ruwach spoke to them without breaking his step. "The Sparks will show you the way."

"Sparks? Is that what they're called?" Brianna said. "Ohhh, I love it!" She cooed at one of the brilliant specks of light that was twinkling merrily and flitting in front of her eyes. "So pretty!" The Spark flew off down a darkened passage and Brianna hurried after it. Xavier, Evan, and Levi followed their own Sparks down other tunnels.

"Come, Prince Manuel!"

Ruwach had almost disappeared from view, so Manuel hurried after him. Despite having to run, Manuel didn't start wheezing or feel the need for his inhaler. *I can breathe,* he thought. He couldn't remember the last time he'd been able to run and breathe effortlessly at the same time. Did this Ruwach fellow have magic powers? What was he anyway? Random questions floated through Manuel's calculating brain. Everything he had seen and heard from the moment he jumped into the tornado had made him question everything he thought he knew about the world. Ahoratos seemed to be a realm of infinite possibilities. He was scared—but excited too.

The darkened tunnel lit up as they moved, and Manuel's attention was soon drawn to the suits of armor that lined the wall. So many varieties, some the likes of which he'd never seen before, some very old-fashioned and some futuristic. There were names and dates listed on each set. He wanted to stop and examine them closer, his scientific brain whirring with theories. But Ruwach did not slow down.

Then, without warning, Ruwach stopped and spun around. Manuel skidded to a halt.

"This is your armor," the guide said, pointing to some objects arrayed on the wall, accompanied by a small placard with his full name and birth date. Manuel stared—it hardly looked like armor at all. Not nearly as impressive as some of the others he'd just passed by. The sword was nice, though, and the shield looked rather grand. The breastplate, however, was nothing but a thin white plate with an orb in the center. The belt and boots were also plain white and unadorned.

"Is that—armor?" he asked, not wanting to offend the guide, who was rather intimidating despite his size.

"Belt first." Ruwach removed the belt from the stand and handed it to Manuel. "Always, belt first."

The belt glowed with some strange symbols as Ruwach held it out, then the symbols disappeared, replaced with a word: *TRUTH*.

"Truth?" Manuel read.

"The belt holds everything together," said Ruwach mysteriously.

Manuel took the belt and looked at it blankly, as the others had done, not sure what to do with it. But when he held it to his waist, it wrapped around him as if it had a will of its own, the two ends melting together.

"Fascinating," he said.

He did the same with the breastplate, wondering at the weirdness of its shape then marveling at how it stuck to his shirt, conforming to his size as if it were made just for him. He tapped on the surface uncertainly.

"Seems rather thin," he remarked. It didn't look like it would stop a sword blow or even a spitball, for that matter. And Manuel knew all about how spitballs felt. "What does this do?" He slid a finger over the orb, as if trying to make it spin.

Ruwach didn't answer, just handed Manuel the boots, which he put on easily. He walked around, trying them out. Brianna had mentioned boots when they were out at the chasm. But Manuel wasn't sure what was so special about these boots, although they were quite different from any shoes he'd ever worn.

"Come," Ruwach commanded and turned swiftly back down the tunnel they had just traveled. Manuel went after him. He wanted to ask about the sword and the other stuff—including the padlocked doors that stood beside each set of armor—but he didn't dare interrupt. He had a feeling that Ruwach didn't tell you anything until you really needed to know.

When they returned to the main room of the Cave, the three boys and Brianna were waiting, dressed much the same as he was. They stood proudly, very pleased with their armor, not at all concerned about its lack of practicality.

"Hey, you look good!" Levi said.

"Thank you," Manuel said skeptically.

"Better check out the rules," said Evan, pointing to a large scroll that had just appeared in the air over their heads. Manuel peered up at the scroll, his lips moving slightly as he read. Most of them he already knew now, like making sure he got to the Water as soon as he arrived in Ahoratos. But there were some he didn't understand.

"Why can't we—" he began, but Ruwach interrupted, his voice booming through the room.

"You have a mission."

Manuel jumped, startled—he was the only one who did so. The others seemed pretty used to that voice.

"A rescue mission."

"A rescue mission?" Evan said. "Didn't we already rescue Levi?"

"Now you must rescue a prisoner of Skot'os," Ruwach said.

"Skot'os!" Evan said. "We can't go over there! We don't even have swords yet."

"You have everything you need."

The kids heard some special emphasis in Ruwach's tone this time, although none of them could put an exact name to it. Maybe Ruwach wasn't talking about *just* the armor anymore.

"Who are we going to rescue?" Levi asked.

"Follow me," Ruwach said. He led them into a room they had never been before, smaller and darker. No glowing stalactites. No Sparks. The only light came from a single lamp stand, under which stood a wooden table. On the table was a small, plain, wooden box.

"Open it," Ruwach said, indicating Xavier. Xavier stepped forward and gingerly opened the box, as if expecting something to pop out. When that didn't happen, he looked inside.

"It's empty," he said, disappointed. All the kids craned their necks to see—the box contained nothing but a purple, satin lining, like the inside of a jewelry box.

"What do you see?" Ruwach asked.

Xavier looked harder. "Well—there *was* something here." He saw that the purple lining was indented—he began to recognize the shape. It was long and narrow, with a knob on one end and a smaller indentation on the other. It reminded him of something he'd seen in a movie once—something sort of old-fashioned but familiar. "Uh, maybe . . . a key?"

Ruwach's hooded head nodded slowly. "The key," he said. "That unlocks the rooms."

"You mean those padlocked rooms we passed?" asked Manuel. Ruwach nodded again.

"What happened to it?" Evan asked.

"It was stolen," Ruwach said.

"By Ponéros?" said Levi.

"By a Prince Warrior of Ahoratos."

The kids were silent, glancing at each other nervously.

"You mean someone—like us?" asked Evan in a small voice.

"We shall call him—Rook. For now." Ruwach extended his hand—it was the first time the kids—other than Levi—had seen it. His hand looked like it was made of light, with no visible creases or lines like a regular hand. He held it palm up, and a beam of swirling white light shot upward from the palm, making the kids shield their eyes for a moment. Ruwach began to tell a story, and as he did, images appeared in the light beam, portraying the tale he told.

"Rook was a fine Prince Warrior, but he was always curious about Skot'os, always going down to the Bridge of Tears to look over the chasm to the other side. He seemed to feel as though there was something there for him, something he was missing on this side of the bridge."

Evan leaned over to his brother, holding his hand to his mouth. "That must be the bridge we saw when we got here," he whispered. Xavier nudged him to be quiet.

The beam from Ruwach's hand showed a Prince Warrior slowly crossing the Bridge of Tears then stopping in the center, where the stone stairway changed to metal beams. Butterflies fluttered merrily around his head, their red eyes blazing, although the warrior did not seem to notice.

"The Ents told him fantastic stories of the wonders of Skot'os," Ruwach said. "The Source continually warned him that they were liars and deceivers, but Rook became more and more taken in by their stories."

"Those insects can talk?" asked Manuel in a soft voice.

"Oh yes, they can," said Brianna with a sigh.

Another figure appeared in the scene—this once much larger, more human-shaped, but very dark and elongated, like a shadow projected against a wall.

"Then, one day, Ponéros came to meet Rook at the bridge. He promised Rook all the riches of Skot'os, a kingdom of his own, if he would steal the key and deliver it to Ponéros in his fortress."

More images appeared—a beautiful castle, mounds of gold, a table filled with food.

"How did Ponéros know about the rooms? Or the key?" Xavier asked.

"He had been in the Cave often, before his rebellion. He knew the secret of the rooms. But he didn't know where the key was hidden."

"Why did Ponéros want the key?" Levi asked.

"He believed that keeping the contents of these rooms hidden from every Prince Warrior was the key to securing his victory in Ahoratos," Ruwach replied. "But he dared not risk coming for it himself. He needed an ally, someone willing to betray us. Rook took the offer. He stole the key and brought it to Ponéros."

The moving picture in the light beam showed Rook, the Prince Warrior, opening the box and pulling out a key. The next image showed Rook handing the key to a shadowy figure.

Evan eyed the string of mysterious, locked doors down the darkened corridors. "So whatever's in those rooms must be really important. What is it, anyway?" He asked the question casually, as if he thought he could trick Ruwach into telling him. Ruwach remained silent. Evan shrugged as if to say, *Well, I tried.*

"So is Rook a king there now?" Levi asked.

"Far from it. He is a prisoner, held in the dungeon in the Fortress of Chaós. He realizes the mistake he made and now begs for his release."

The vision of the beautiful castle returned—but then it changed before the kids' eyes, the fine stone walls and turrets melting away, leaving only a disordered skeleton of metal beams and girders. The colors of the gardens and the surrounding landscape smeared together in an ugly stew, like when you mix too many paints at once. The whole picture was one of desolation and sorrow.

Then the vision faded completely. Ruwach drew his hand back into his robe. The kids were all silent a long moment, disturbed by the story they had just heard and seen.

"So you want *us* to go there—to that fortress—and rescue Rook?" Xavier said at length. "But why? He betrayed you. He stole from you. He's getting the punishment he deserves."

"You didn't leave *me* when I got stuck," Levi said.

"That's different—"

"No, it isn't. Right, Ru?" Levi looked meaningfully at the guide.

Ruwach's hood nodded slowly. "You wear the shoes of peace. To bring the good news to the prisoners who need to be set free. And every prisoner should have the chance to experience freedom."

"How can news set a prisoner free?" Evan asked, scrunching his eyebrows. "Don't we need saws to cut the bars? Or dynamite? And swords to fight the guards?"

"You need only this." Ruwach produced from his robes a small scroll, sealed with the Crest of Ahoratos. He handed it to Levi. "Guard it carefully until you give it to the one who needs to be set free."

Levi took the scroll, smirking a little that he was chosen to carry it. He placed it carefully in his pocket.

Ruwach nodded.

"What about our instructions?" said Xavier.

"Ah." Ruwach raised his long arms toward a dark corner of the room. It lit up, revealing a long, straight passageway, at the end of which was a shining object the kids instantly recognized.

"The Book!" said Brianna.

The Book sped toward them as Ruwach drew it in. This time it was Manuel who ducked for cover, certain it would crash into them. The other kids stifled their laughter, all but Evan, who laughed out loud.

"Did you see him duck?" he said.

"Yeah, I seem to remember you doing the same thing," Xavier said, flicking him on the back of his head.

Manuel peeked out from under his arms and stared in wide-eyed awe at the golden book flickering before him on the fancy pedestal. "Oh my," he said. "I've never seen a hologram this realistic."

"That's because it isn't a hologram," said Levi.

Ruwach approached The Book and lifted one robed arm over it—the pages began flipping and then stopped. Words lifted off the page and reassembled in midair above The Book:

Look straight ahead, and fix your
eyes on what lies before you.

The words hovered a moment before Ruwach seemed to pull them out of the air and fling them into each of the orbs on the kids' breastplates, where they spun around, making the orbs glow. Manuel tapped on his orb, trying to figure out how it worked.

"This is a new projection technology I haven't seen before," he said. "I wish I had my notebook—"

Ruwach began flipping pages again. All the kids watched, breathless, as a new set of instructions poured out of the Book, unscrambling in the air before them.

Take hold of my instructions; don't let them go.
Guard them, for they are the key to life.

"Whose instructions?" said Manuel.

"The Source," said Brianna. "That's who wrote The Book."

"But what *are* the instructions?" asked Xavier, still not understanding. "Like, how do we get to Skot'os, for instance? And how do we get into the fortress?"

"Yeah, and how do we *not* get caught and turned into Forgers?" said Brianna.

"Your armor will guide you," said Ruwach placidly, as if unconcerned about their worries.

"I *really* think we will need more equipment," Manuel said nervously. "If we are going to go into enemy territory—I mean, there might be guards with swords and spears and perhaps artillery—"

The kids all talked at once, raising every objection they could think of.

"Remember, you wear the shoes of peace," Ruwach said in his thundering voice, bringing them to silence. "Trust your armor. You have everything you need."

With that, Ruwach—and the Cave—were gone.

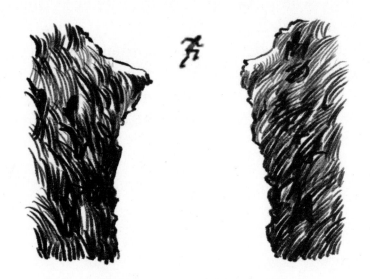

CHAPTER TWENTY-ONE

Building Bridges

The five kids found themselves standing once again at the edge of the great chasm with the rushing stream below. The landscape on the other side was still shrouded in dense fog. The red sky was streaked with purple and hung with those bizarre skypods that they had seen before.

"Where's the bridge?" Levi said. It took them all a moment to realize that the Bridge of Tears—which they had seen plainly when they had first landed—was gone.

"Ruwach didn't tell us that the bridge was gone!" Evan said.

"Maybe Ponéros knew we would be coming," said Xavier. "So he took out the only access we had."

"How could he know?" Brianna asked. "Could he hear us talking in the Cave?"

"Perhaps he—or one of his spies—saw us land here and went to tell Ponéros, and he just got suspicious," said Manuel, reasoning things out as he always did. "At any rate, the bridge is gone, so until Ruwach builds another one, we will not be going to Skot'os today. Which is a relief, to tell you the truth. I really did not want to venture over there on my first day here." Manuel pushed up his glasses and smiled crookedly. "We need a new plan."

"I'm with Manuel," Evan added. "I say we head to the castle, grab some ice cream, and come up with a new plan."

Xavier rolled his eyes. "Our instructions were to follow the instructions," he said. "Which means doing what Ruwach sent us here to do."

"But how?" said Levi. "Should we climb down there and up the other side? Or jump like we did before?"

Xavier looked down at the water thoughtfully, then shook his head. "The Crest isn't there. So I don't think we should jump."

"If we had some rappelling gear it might be feasible," said Manuel, "or some materials whereby I could fashion a flying machine—"

"A flying machine?" Levi said, laughing. "Seriously?"

"Well, I almost had one working at home—until my father took it away. Too dangerous, he said." Manuel shrugged, as if he still didn't understand the problem.

"I read this book once where the hero threw a rope over a river and it caught on the other side, and then the characters zip-lined over," Brianna said. "Maybe we could use our belts to do that."

"That wouldn't work," said Evan with a roll of his eyes.

"Actually, it's not a bad idea," said Xavier. "It's worth a try anyway."

Brianna gave Evan a *so-there* look, which he did his best to ignore.

"Give me your belts," Xavier said. They each took off their belts and handed them to Xavier.

"There's no way it will be long enough to go all the way across," Manuel said, shaking his head.

"Oh, you haven't seen these belts in action," said Brianna with a smile.

Xavier touched the ends of the belts together. They fused into one, long, continuous belt, much to Manuel's astonishment. But still, he shook his head.

"Still not long enough."

Xavier gathered the belt up into a loop, like a cowboy does before roping a calf. He took a big breath and threw it across the chasm with all his strength. The belt unfurled, sailing through the air . . . then dropped down over the cliff edge.

Manuel sniffed. "I thought so."

"Try again," said Brianna.

Xavier tried again and again. But the belt-rope failed to make it all the way across the chasm, let alone grab onto something on the other side.

"That didn't work," said Evan, glancing sideways at Brianna, who avoided his gaze.

"I guess that means we aren't supposed to use the belts," said Xavier. He unhitched the belts and returned them to the others, who fastened them around their waists once more.

"Now what?" said Levi. "Maybe we could cut down some of these tall trees and lash them together with the belts and lay them across . . ."

"What are we going to cut down trees with?" said Evan.

While they continued to discuss ideas, Xavier gazed thoughtfully over the edge of the cliff to the stream. The instructions from The Book rolled over and over in his head. The orb in his breastplate seemed to know what he was thinking, for the words beamed out and floated in the air before him: *Look straight ahead. Fix your eyes on what is before you.*

He looked up, toward the other side of the chasm. He saw something, just a flicker at first, then it grew steadier. A light. Shining through the thick fog on the other side.

You wear the shoes of peace.

Ruwach's words tumbled in his head. He looked down at his boots. Then he turned to the other kids and exclaimed, "The shoes!"

They stopped talking and looked at him, startled by his outburst. Xavier's face seemed to shine.

"Remember what Ruwach said just before he disappeared? *You wear the shoes of peace.* It's the *shoes* that will get us across!"

"Really?" said Brianna doubtfully. She looked down at her boots. Although still rather sparkly, they did not seem to be doing anything special at the moment. "Are they going to fly us there?" All the kids examined their boots, hoping to see them sprouting wings.

Xavier set his jaw and moved to the lip of the cliff, where the bridge had once stood. He gazed over the edge—it was a long, *long* way down.

Fix your eyes. The voice was stronger, louder. Ruwach's voice? Calling him to look up, to focus. He looked to the light flickering through the fog on the other side of the chasm. The others were silent, watching him. He took a deep breath.

"Xavi! What are you doing?" Evan cried. He went to grab his brother's arm. But it was too late. Xavier had already lifted one foot in the air, as if he was about to ascend a staircase that wasn't there.

———————

Xavier kept his eyes on the light as he stepped up, not wanting to look down at the deep ravine below. The breath he had taken was locked in his chest as his foot descended. But then it stopped. On . . . *something*. He glanced down quickly. A stone. The step of a stairway that hadn't been there a moment before. He let the air rush out of his chest in relief.

"Look!" he heard Evan shout behind him. "That step just appeared under his foot!"

Xavier let his lungs fill with air again, nearly laughing with relief and joy when he looked down and saw the stone step hovering under his outstretched foot. He stuck both arms out to steady himself and gain his composure. "Look straight ahead!" he shouted. "See the light? Fix your eyes on what lies before you!"

He took another breath and another step—and another stone appeared under his foot, floating in the air yet perfectly solid. But as soon as he lifted his other foot off the first step, it disappeared. It was as if the steps only became visible when the boot was actually touching it.

The others laughed and cheered, thrilled by Xavier's discovery.

"It's amazing!" said Brianna.

"Cool," said Levi.

"Kind of like *Minecraft*," said Manuel. Being the scientist, he had to know how this worked. He picked up a large pebble and knelt down at the edge of the cliff. "Maybe the steps are there, we just can't see them." He tossed the pebble out onto the space where Xavier's first step had appeared. But the pebble didn't hit anything. It just dropped all the way down to the ravine below.

"Whoa!" said Evan, watching. "The step just disappeared!"

Xavier took another step, creating yet another stone under his foot. "Come on, guys!"

"Let's do this!" Brianna said. "We have to hurry before any bad guys see us."

"I don't think so," Manuel said. "I'm sort of afraid of heights—"

"This will cure you!" Brianna stepped up to the cliff edge and focused her gaze on the light shining on the other side. Staring at the light made her feel calmer.

She repeated the words in her head: *Fix your eyes on what lies before you.* She took a deep breath and stuck one foot into the air. For a heart-stopping moment she thought she might tumble all the way down to the rocky stream below, but then her foot stopped on something solid. She glanced down quickly and saw a stone under her boot. She shrieked with delight.

"It's working!"

Levi went next, followed quickly by Evan. They also whooped victoriously as the steps appeared under their boots, allowing them to walk up the stairway, right over the top of the chasm.

"Don't look down!" Xavier called out. "Just keep looking at that light!"

"Come on Manuel," Levi said, beckoning him. "You can do it!"

Manuel stood on the edge and wrung his hands nervously. "Maybe I'll just wait here," he mumbled.

"Come on, Manuel! It's fun!" said Brianna, jumping one-footed from one step to the next like she was playing hopscotch. The others laughed. They seemed to forget about the deadly rocks far below them and the enemy territory ahead of them, as they delighted in the newfound power of their boots.

They were almost to the center when Xavier remembered how the bridge had looked different on the other side. Would the steps now change to metal beams, making them slip and fall? He began to wonder if there were spies of the enemy on the other side, watching them, setting a trap. Other than the light, it was impossible to see anything in the fog. He thought he heard something—a fluttering noise, there and gone again.

"Hey, guys, quiet!" he hissed at the other kids. They stopped talking and laughing. "Listen."

For a moment there was no sound but a mournful wind. The kids followed Xavier's gaze, looking straight ahead at the light shining out of the fog bank. Xavier took a long breath.

"Okay, maybe it was nothing," he said. "But let's be quiet, okay? We don't need to call attention to ourselves."

Xavier took another step—but before his boot could create another stone, the fog bank burst into motion, as if it had come alive. He knew instantly what it was.

"Ents!" he shouted to the others. He stood still as the deadly horde advanced. The collective sound was a high-pitched wail that chilled him to his very bones. He raised his hands as if in readiness for their attack. "Don't look away from the light!" he commanded, but he doubted the others could even hear his voice.

"Ahhh!" shrieked Brianna, ducking, her hands flying over her face as the Ents swarmed over them, turning the very air above them into a sea of gray, beating wings.

"Bean!" Levi shouted. He was behind her and could see her stone already fading because she was no longer looking at the light. He batted away the horrible butterflies, struggling to keep his focus, at the same time reaching forward to grab Brianna before her stone disappeared.

"Bean! Look ahead!"

Brianna opened her eyes and tried to focus on the light. She teetered a bit before regaining her balance, her step reappearing. Levi took a breath of relief. But then he heard a cry behind him—Evan was so distracted by the Ents that when he tried to take a step, there was no stone under his foot at all. He started falling and screamed in terror, lurching forward and clutching at one of Levi's boots. He managed to hang on with one arm, his body dangling helplessly. Levi reached down to grab Evan's arm as it clutched his boot, still trying to stay focused on the light.

"Evan!" shouted Levi. "Hang on!" Evan threw his other arm around Levi's boot, swinging his legs up to catch the stone. But he couldn't get a foothold.

"Help!" Evan cried.

Brianna reached back to grab Levi's belt, to give him more leverage, flailing at the Ents with her free arm. "Go away!" she yelled. She took her eyes off the light as she fought the Ents, and her step began to fade. She cried out, wobbling dangerously.

Xavier stole a glance behind him and saw Brianna about to fall. He reached back to steady her.

"Look up!" he shouted. Then he took a step backward—to the step Brianna was on. It began to solidify. Brianna righted herself, gasping. "Don't look at the Ents, and don't look down, whatever you do," he told her. She nodded, refocusing, steadying her breathing. She took a step forward to the next stone.

Xavier knew Evan was in trouble. And he would have to turn his back on the light in order to help him. "Hang on, Van!" he shouted. He took a breath, then spun around and crouched low, reaching out his hand to Evan, whose arms had begun to slip from Levi's boots.

"Take my hand!" Xavier shouted to his brother. "Hurry!"

"I—can't—" Evan sputtered, shaking his head and shutting his eyes.

"Take my hand!" Xavier shouted again. "Now!"

Evan gulped down air. If he let go of Levi's boot he was more than likely to lose his grip altogether and fall straight down onto the rocks below. He stared at Xavier's outstretched arm hovering a foot away. He saw Xavier's stone fading rapidly. In another moment the stone would disappear and he would fall . . .

It was now or never.

Evan let go of the boot and grabbed onto Xavier's hand. Xavier, with a strength born of pure desperation, dragged Evan up and across Levi's step to his own, at the same time spinning them both around to face the light.

"Look up!" Xavier said. Evan raised his head, focusing on the light, trying to ignore the dive-bombing Ents. The step began to strengthen again, solid enough for them both to stand on.

Levi slumped forward, exhaling air he'd been holding far too long.

"You okay?" Xavier asked. Evan regained his balance, sucking in breaths, his face very pale.

"Thanks," he said, his voice cracking.

Xavier put a hand on his shoulder, reassuring him. "Keep going," he said. "Stay focused. The Ents can't hurt you, as long as you fix your eyes on the light."

Evan nodded and took another step, a new stone appearing under his foot. Xavier watched him, breathing deep, forcing air deep into his lungs. His chest felt curiously tight.

"Levi?" he said.

"Yeah, I'm good," Levi said, his voice breathless but sure. "But Manuel is still on the other side."

Xavier sighed. "You go with Evan," he said. "I'll go back for him." He waited until Levi had passed him and was headed over the bridge. Then he steadied himself and called out: "Manuel?"

"I'm here!" said a frail voice. Xavier took a quick glance behind him and saw Manuel back on the cliff. "I think I'll just wait here until you guys get back. I can be the lookout."

"Manuel! You need to stay with us!" Xavier said, exasperated. "Come on! Just keep your eyes on the light on the other side and you'll be fine."

"No thank you! I'm really sorry. But I can't do it."

Xavier stood a moment, pondering what to do. Should he leave Manuel behind? He was tempted. Manuel probably wouldn't be much help on this mission, and he might even be a big liability. Maybe it would be better if he just stayed at the bridge and waited.

But Manuel had received the same instructions as the rest of them. He had to come. There must be a reason. Xavier didn't know what it was, but he knew he had to get Manuel to cross the chasm.

Xavier could see the other kids moving forward steadily, doing their best to ignore the swooping Ents. They would be okay. He sighed. Keeping his focus on the light, he began backing up slowly, trusting that the steps he needed to stand on would be there. Ents flew at him, their red eyes flaring, taunting him. But they didn't shoot darts. They were just trying to distract him from the light. He tried not to think about the rushing water and boulders below.

Fix your eyes . . .

By the time he made it back to where Manuel stood, the others were nearly all the way to the other side. That was a relief anyway.

"Manuel," Xavier said, standing on the first step of the bridge. "Come on. I'll help you. The Ents can't hurt you, so long as you keep your eyes on the light."

"How do you know that?"

"I just do," said Xavier. "Look, it's just like before, when you jumped. You were fine, right?"

"I . . . suppose so . . ."

"Just do it again. Your boots will carry you. But *you* have to do the walking." Xavier took another step up, a stone appearing under his foot. "Fix your eyes."

Manuel strained to gaze at the light on the other side. He found that once he did that, he didn't really notice the horrid, flapping bugs quite so much. He took a deep breath and adjusted his glasses. And took a step.

One . . .

And then another.

Two . . .

He counted as he walked behind Xavier up the steps to the middle, where they started to descend to the other side.

Twenty-five, twenty-six, twenty-seven . . .

He counted, focused on the light. Ents flew around his head, but he continued to ignore them. Xavier was right—they couldn't hurt him as long as he didn't look at them. He smiled to himself, straightening his shoulders, quickening his step. He counted all the way to forty-seven before he realized he'd made it. The other kids began to cheer (quietly) as he stepped off the last stone and onto the solid ground.

"That wasn't so bad, was it?" said Levi, patting him on the back.

"I guess not," Manuel said, grinning broadly now. He turned to Xavier. "Thank you. For helping me."

Xavier shrugged, grinning back. Then he turned to examine the surroundings. He couldn't see anything except fog.

"Skot'os is pretty foggy," said Evan, mostly to himself.

"The light," Brianna said, "the one we followed—where is it?" The kids searched through the compact gray blanket for a glimmer of light—and of hope.

The light was gone. The fog was so enveloping they could not even see the chasm or the Ents anymore. They felt it thickening, closing in on them, as if seeping into their skin. They started to turn in different directions, panic overtaking them as they realized they had lost all sense of direction. One wrong move and they might end up falling into the chasm.

"What do we do?" Manuel said, voicing the fear they were all feeling but didn't want to admit.

Xavier took a breath, trying to think.

Chaos. Confusion. Ruwach had described them as the trademarks of Ponéros. The enemy wanted them to be confused. That's what this fog was about.

But they had the armor. The breastplate. He remembered standing in the sandstorm, waiting for the breastplate to tell him what to do. Sometimes it took awhile—they had to be patient.

"Just hang on, everyone," Xavier said. "Stay calm. Just—wait."

He looked down at his own breastplate, waiting, breathing. The others did as well.

After what seemed like an eternity, their breastplates flickered with a gentle light. Xavier let out a breath he'd been holding and began turning until the light became steady. The others did the same. Unlike the last time they were together, their breastplates all pointed in the same direction.

"Levi, you have that scroll?" Xavier asked.

"Yeah," Levi said. He pulled the scroll out of his pocket. "I got it."

"Good," Xavier said. "Follow me. Be as quiet as possible." No one argued with him, not even Evan. He'd gotten them over the bridge. Without anyone saying it out loud, they'd made him their leader.

"If you see anyone," Levi said, "don't talk to them. And don't even look at them. Especially . . ." he looked down momentarily, "if they look—familiar."

Xavier nodded to him. "Right."

CHAPTER TWENTY-TWO

Chaós

They walked quietly through the fog, in single file, not speaking at all. They could make out no features of the landscape. The only sound was the occasional whine and flutter of the Ents, which seemed to be tracking them from above, invisible.

Xavier stayed focused on the breastplate guiding him, whispering encouragements to the others from time to time. Evan stayed close behind him, followed by Brianna, then Levi, then Manuel. None of them spoke, concentrating on the person in front of them, making sure the light of their breastplates remained steady. The ground beneath their feet was soft and sticky, like thick mud. But at least it felt somewhat solid and they weren't sinking.

Gradually the fog began to lighten, and weird objects came into view: colorful, odd-shaped flowers with clownlike faces that sprouted and withered randomly, and black trees whose bare limbs twisted around each other in crazy patterns, entangling in the branches of others. Xavier stopped when a large, red-and-green animal darted across their path. It looked like a robotic version of a dog, with big red buttons for eyes, a tin can for a snout, and a long, segmented tail.

"What *was* that thing?" asked Evan, gazing into the fog where the "dog" had disappeared.

Xavier had no idea. Confusion. This was a world of confusion, where nothing made any sense.

Large, lumpy objects began to appear along the path as they walked. They were like rocks, but different too—spongy, not hard. Brianna tripped over one and it caught her boot, sucking it in. She gasped, yanking her foot away quickly.

"That rock!" she said, panting. "It tried to grab me!"

"Don't go near them, stay on the path," Xavier said. Above them the Ents wheeled in relentless circles below a red-purple sky.

The ground dipped down into a narrow ravine, but instead of water at the bottom, the kids saw a thick green substance jiggling like Jell-O. They stopped, watching. Evan bent to put a finger in it, to see if it really was Jell-O.

"Don't!" Xavier said sharply. "Jump over it. Don't touch it." He knew that nothing in this land could be trusted. He crouched down and jumped with both feet, his boots taking him safely over the Jell-O stream to the mucky ground on the other side. The other kids followed his lead, all landing safely.

"Makes me hungry," Evan mumbled. The other kids looked at him. He shrugged. "What? I like Jell-O!"

They climbed up out of the ravine and then stopped again, confronted by a complicated web of steel girders blocking their path. The ground itself seemed to have disappeared, replaced by metal beams crisscrossing in random patterns, suspended in space. Xavier hesitated, his breastplate blinking a warning.

"What is it?" asked Levi.

None of them knew. They were surrounded by a complex maze of steel girders, like the inside of a roller coaster or an unfinished skyscraper. Remnants of the angry sky shone through here and there, as did the shadow of a huge skypod that loomed overhead.

"I think this might be the entrance to the fortress," said Xavier. Then, under his breath: "Chaós."

He looked down as his breastplate began to glow steadily, pointing straight ahead. "Okay, we're going in."

"In there?" said Manuel, his voice shaky.

Xavier nodded. "Follow in my footsteps. Stay close."

Xavier picked his way carefully through the warren of girders, stopping often to make sure the others were following. The breastplate changed directions frequently and unexpectedly. Sometimes they walked along a beam, balancing like tightrope walkers, and other times they jumped from one beam to the next, trying to avoid looking down at the black void below them. At one point Xavier paused and looked up again—the maze of girders was growing taller, the girders lengthening, twisting, and turning around each other, reaching into the red, bruised sky.

Soon the web of girders blocked out all available light. The kids were enveloped in darkness, seeking their way with nothing but the breastplates to guide them. They huddled closer together, inching along at a snail's pace, uncertain of what lay ahead.

"I'm not crazy about this," Brianna mumbled uneasily.

"Me neither," said Xavier. "But we need to keep—"

He froze when he heard a new noise, the sound of rhythmic, pounding footsteps. He held up a hand and the kids stopped. Something was moving directly in front of them. He waited, holding his breath, his heartbeat loud in his own ears.

A shadow passed by, attached to a large, slow-moving creature made entirely of metal with red, glowing orbs for eyes.

Forger.

It looked much like the creature that had trapped Levi but larger, its massive body encased in rusty metal plates of various colors riveted together. Its helmet-like head was small in comparison to the rest of its body, but the eyes shone like lasers, piercing the darkness.

Xavier stood perfectly still, willing the others to do the same. The Forger's gaze swept slowly in both directions. After an agonizing moment it began moving again, its steps slow but heavy, making the girders around it shiver. Xavier waited until the Forger passed them by, its echoing steps receding. He let out a long breath. It hadn't seen them.

Then Manuel sneezed.

He'd been holding it for as long as he could, but he just couldn't hold it anymore. Levi whipped around and stared at him. Manuel mouthed the word *sorry*.

But it was too late. The Forger spun around, its laser beam eyes zeroing in on them.

"Run!" Xavier shouted. He sprinted away, leading the others on a mad scramble through the maze of girders, the thundering steps of the Forger growing ever nearer. They came to a long, metal staircase that descended into darkness below. "This way!" he ordered as he tore down the steps, taking them two at a time, his boots clanging noisily against the metal surface. The others followed as quickly as they could. Manuel stumbled and nearly knocked Levi over. "Sorry!" he whispered again. Levi recovered his balance—being a skateboarder came in handy sometimes—and grabbed Manuel before he fell all the way down.

When Xavier reached the bottom he saw a large steel door in front of him. He grabbed the metal handle and pulled. It didn't move. Locked.

Dead end.

The breastplates went dark.

CHAPTER TWENTY-THREE

The Key to Freedom

Xavier yanked the door handle again and again, but it wouldn't budge. He turned, pressing his back to the door, facing the others as they came down the steps.

"It's locked," he said.

"Are you sure you followed the armor?" Levi asked, panting.

"I thought I did—" *I did. Didn't I?* Xavier tried to think. They had been moving so fast, and the breastplate

239

had changed directions a lot—perhaps he took a wrong turn?

There was no time to think about it. The Forger had made it to the stairs and was coming down, each step an echoing boom, radiating into the kids' very souls.

"Ruwach . . ." Brianna whispered, pleading for their guide to come and help them. She inched closer to Levi, her fingers gripping his sleeve. The others huddled closer together, preparing for the worst.

"I'm sorry," Manuel whispered. "This is all my fault. If I hadn't sneezed—"

"Shh," said Evan.

The red glowing eyes focused on the kids as the Forger clomped down the steps. It seemed to be taking its time, as if it enjoyed making the kids tremble. Brianna whimpered a little, turning her face away so she couldn't see. The Forger came closer, stretching out one metal arm toward Brianna, its fingers straightening.

Xavier knew that one touch from the Forger and Brianna would start to turn into metal. *But if it just touched me,* he thought, *then she—and the others— might have time to get away. He can't grab us all at the same time.* He was surprised that what he felt was less like fear and more like a need to protect his friends, give them a chance to escape. He stepped in front of Brianna and moved toward the Forger.

"Xavi!" whispered Evan, seeing what he was doing. The others gasped. But Xavier kept moving into the path of the Forger. He saw the metal hand reaching now toward him.

"Run!" he whispered to his friends. He shut his eyes, waiting for the cold, hard touch of the Forger's fingers to graze his skin.

It never did.

After a moment, Xavier opened his eyes and saw small twinkling puffs of light flitting around the Forger's face like mosquitoes. *Sparks.* The Forger shook its head violently, its glowing eyes spinning in circles to track their movement. The Sparks seemed to be leaving light trails in intricate patterns as they danced around the Forger's metal head. The patterns were beautiful and everchanging in a myriad of colors—the Forger was mesmerized by them.

Manuel gaped at the spectacle of the Forger and the Sparks. But then he noticed something dangling from the Forger's thick metal belt—it was long and black, with a kind of scrolled handle, like one of those ornate iron gates in front of fancy houses. It was different from everything else he'd seen in Skot'os so far—it had delicacy, symmetry . . . even beauty.

And then he realized what it was.

A key.

The instruction from The Book mentioned something about a key. And Ruwach had said a key had been stolen. Maybe *this* was the key he'd been talking about. Maybe this key opened the door of the prison.

He glanced at the others—none of them seemed to notice the key. They were all focused on the Sparks. Xavier was still frozen in place, the Forger's finger inches from his face. Manuel took a deep breath, gathering his courage, then began to creep toward the Forger.

He tripped, falling forward over the Forger's large armored boot. His glasses flew off his face and clattered against its leg. He held his breath, sure he would be caught in the Forger's deadly grip. But it seemed not to notice. The Sparks had woven a net of light around its head.

"What are you doing?" whispered Xavier, watching him out of the corner of his eye. He didn't move a muscle, aware that any movement might draw the Forger's attention away from the Sparks.

"The key—" Manuel said, pointing upward in the vague direction of the belt. When he looked up, he realized he could see the key perfectly well. He could see everything, in fact. *Without his glasses.*

"Can you reach it?" Xavier asked, still in a very soft voice.

Manuel nodded with new confidence, stepped over the Forger's boot, and snatched the key off its belt. It was a lot heavier than he supposed, and Manuel fumbled a moment, nearly dropping it. Yet the Forger took no notice of him. Manuel waited another moment to be sure, then scrambled back to the others.

"I got it!" he said, holding the key up so Xavier could see it.

"Try it in the door!" Levi said in a hushed voice.

"First, get your glasses," Xavier murmured.

"But I don't need them—"

"You can't leave anything behind. It's one of the rules."

Manuel remembered reading that on the scroll in the Cave. He nodded and went to retrieve his glasses, lying right next to the Forger's boot. There was a big crack in one of the lenses. He stuck them in his pocket for safekeeping.

"Okay," Xavier whispered slowly. "Now open the door."

Manuel crept over to the door and jammed the key into the padlock. For one awful second he was sure it wouldn't fit, but then he jiggled it and finally it turned, the lock snapping open.

"I got it!"

"Go on," said Xavier. "Go through the door, all of you. I'll follow you."

Manuel heaved on the heavy door. The others joined in to help. The door scraped against the floor and squealed loudly in protest, as if it hadn't been opened in a very long time. The sound caught the attention of the Forger, whose head swiveled toward them, its red eyes spinning crazily, still blinded by the web of light created by the Sparks. Its arms began to flail about, searching for the source of the noise.

"Quick!" said Xavier. "Go through!" He spun around, ducking to avoid the Forger's thrashing arms, as the others rushed to the open door. Once they were all through, Xavier turned and slipped through the door, pulling out the key as he did so and shutting it tightly behind him. He slid the key into his boot for safekeeping.

"Let's hope the Sparks can keep that guy busy for a while," he said with a deep sigh.

He saw that they were in a long, narrow room lined with cages, eerily lit by dozens of green-glowing light-bulbs dangling from a high ceiling. The walls dripped with something slimy and fetid, and the air smelled of dead things.

"It's the prison," said Evan. His voice did not echo at all, the sound deadened by the heavy gloom of the place.

"Rook is in here somewhere," Levi said.

"It's gross," Brianna said. "Stinky."

"But there are so many cells!" Evan said. "How are we going to know which one Rook is in?"

"We'll have to look in every cell," Xavier said. "Levi, you, Manuel, and Brianna take that side, and Evan and I will take this side. Call out if you find him. Better hurry too. There's probably more of those Forgers around this place."

The prisoners stared at the young warriors as they filed past. Some were completely metal, like the Forger. Others seemed more human, only parts of their bodies metal-ized—arms, legs, torsos. They all had shackles around their ankles and wrists, so when they moved, the chains scraped on the floor and echoed against the walls.

Levi walked from cell to cell, gazing into the faces of each of the prisoners. The light from his breastplate reflected in their eyes—most seemed empty, pupil-less, as if their souls had deserted them. Even the ones that still had human skin stared at him blankly, devoid of emotion. Others just growled or moaned. Levi wasn't afraid—he felt sorry for them.

He passed by one prisoner but then stopped, turning back. This one was mostly metal—only the fingers of one hand were still flesh. But its eyes were different. They were tender, human, not hollow and wasted. They looked back at Levi with something like sorrow. Levi saw several streaks on the prisoner's metal face— he realized they were the tracks of tears.

He remembered his own tears when he was stuck in the dome, turning to metal. How full of remorse he had been, for himself, for what he had done. He hadn't been able to escape—but he *had* been able to cry.

"Hey, guys," Levi said softly, "I think I found him."

"You did?" Brianna said, going over to him.

Levi looked between the bars, studying the face before him. "Are you Rook?" he asked. The other kids had gathered to stare at the prisoner, who rose and limped toward them, dragging his chains. He grasped the cell bars, pressing his metal face between them. A fresh tear fell down his rusted cheek.

"You c-c-c . . ." the prisoner's voice crackled, like he hadn't used it in a very long time. He shook his head and tried again. "You came, for me?"

Levi took the scroll from his pocket and held it out. Rook stared at it blankly for only a moment before he reached to grasp it with his human fingers. It shook in his hand. He pressed it against his metal hand for leverage and cracked the seal, unrolling the scroll and reading the contents.

Once freed, always free.

"Free?" Rook whispered. "I am . . . *free?*"

Levi nodded. He smiled tentatively at the prisoner, as if to reassure him. "Ruwach told us to bring you that message."

Evan, Brianna, Xavier, and Manuel each nodded a greeting to Rook, who looked from one to the other in astonishment, unable to speak. He read the scroll again. *Once freed, always free.* He shook his head in disbelief.

"I didn't think I could ever be free again . . ." His voice sounded squeaky, like a hinge in need of oil. He lowered his head, and the kids saw more tears fall from his eyes, creating more rusty streaks on his metal face. "I never thought anyone would come for me."

Xavier pulled the key out of his boot and handed it to Levi, who stuck it in the lock on the prisoner's door. He turned it, and it clicked a few times before the door creaked open.

"The chains!" Manuel said.

"This key won't fit in those locks," said Xavier, holding the key close to one of Rook's shackles. "It's way too big."

"Maybe there's a saw or hammer or something down here we can use," said Evan. The kids began hunting around for something heavy that would break the chains. Levi just stood motionless, staring at the scroll in Rook's metal hand.

"Ruwach said that that scroll was all you would need to be free," he said finally. "Use *it*."

"But how?"

Levi wasn't sure. He just chose to believe what Ruwach had said anyway. Without warning, the scroll began to turn red, like it had caught fire.

"Hey, look!" Levi said, pointing. Rook looked down at the scroll and dropped it, jumping away in alarm. A thin ribbon of smoke wafted up from one end of the scroll.

Just then Levi had an idea. "Use the scroll!" he said. "Use it on the chains!"

Rook hesitated but then clumsily picked up the smoldering scroll with his metal hand and pressed it against one of the shackles around his wrist. The iron began to turn red, heating up as if the scroll was actually melting it. The kids gathered at the bars to watch in awe as the scroll—made of paper—sizzled and melted the heavy shackle around Rook's wrist until it broke open and fell away.

"Whoa," said Evan.

Rook could not hide his excitement. He pressed the burning scroll to the other wrist iron, watching it melt and fall away as the first one had. He spread his arms wide, just because he could, and let out a soft cry of joy. For a sacred moment, gladness wafted through the dank hollow halls of the dungeon.

It was cut off by a pounding on the door of the prison, so loud and fearsome it made the green bulbs shiver on their chains. The kids looked up, shrinking away in sudden fear.

"Forgers," Xavier said. "Sounds like a bunch of them. They found us."

"Quick! Your legs!" Levi said. Rook hurried to burn away the leg shackles with the scroll, but it took an agonizingly long time. The commotion grew louder, and the lightbulbs quaked and swung about, some of them breaking, causing an explosion of sparks. The kids ducked to avoid being hit with glass shards.

"We need to get out of here," Manuel said over and over, his arms over his head.

Rook stepped through the open door of his prison cell. "Thank you," he whispered, trying to smile despite the metal of his face. "Thank you. For coming to get me."

The door suddenly seemed to explode off its hinges. Voices like growling dogs echoed throughout the prison chamber. It was hard to see anything, for very few of the lightbulbs were still burning.

"Can't get out that way," Xavier said, indicating the door.

"We're doomed!" wailed Manuel.

"I know another way out," whispered Rook. "Follow me!"

Xavier grabbed the key from the cell door and with the others followed Rook to the far end of the prison. It seemed at first like another dead end, but then Rook knelt down and felt around on the floor with his good hand, mumbling to himself. Finally, he found what he was looking for: a lid, like a sewer cover.

"Here it is!" he said. "Can you help me? I can't do it alone . . ."

The boys crouched down to pull up the round iron cover from the floor and push it aside. They looked down into the hole. Some sort of black slimy muck moved slowly below. It did not look the least bit inviting. But all their breastplates lit up, pointing the way down.

"What is that gunk?" Brianna asked.

"It's sludge," Rook said. "From the fortress. The tunnel empties into the chasm."

"Gross."

"I'll go first."

"Good idea," said Brianna.

Rook positioned himself over the hole, which was difficult with his metal body. Then he jumped. The kids saw him fall and heard him make a squishing noise as he landed. "It's all right!" he yelled. "Jump!"

One by one they jumped down, Xavier waiting until last. He could see the Forgers approaching, hear their snarling voices as they rattled the cages of the prisoners, searching for the intruders. Xavier looked at the iron cover—he wouldn't be able to move it back over the hole and jump down at the same time. The Forgers would see where they went, eventually. But there wasn't much he could do about that.

Xavier dropped into the thick muck of the tunnel. He sank up to his ankles. The horrible sound of the Forgers echoed against the metal walls of the prison above. Brianna covered her ears.

"We need to go this way!" said Rook in a loud whisper, pointing in one direction.

"No, this way," said Brianna, pointing the opposite way. "We have to follow the armor."

"No, no—that will lead to the chasm!" Rook said. "You don't want to go that way. It's a dead end!"

"Well, we *are* going that way," said Evan. "You want to come with us or not?"

Rook tried to argue, but it was no use. The kids' minds were made up. He followed them down the mucky tunnel, which twisted and turned several times before it ended, as he knew it would, at a culvert that emptied into the chasm over the rushing stream far below.

"I told you this was the wrong way!" said Rook. "There's no way out here! If we go back the other way, we might be able to get out and make it to the bridge—"

"There is no bridge anymore," said Levi.

"No bridge?" said Rook, not understanding. "Then how did you get here?"

The kids stood together at the edge of the culvert, looking toward the cliff on the other side. Rook had no idea what they were doing.

"What's going on?" he asked. They seemed to be waiting for something. He followed their gazes, but he saw nothing.

"Up there!" said Evan, pointing. Rook looked toward where he was pointing, at a small, flickering light shining out from the edge of the cliff on the other side.

Then, to his horror, he saw Evan take a step off the ledge into the chasm.

"Stop!" he shouted. But too late—except that Evan didn't fall down. A stone step had appeared under his foot. He continued to step up like he was going up a set of invisible stairs, and the stones continued to appear. Xavier and Brianna quickly followed in Evan's footsteps. Manuel did the same thing. Rook was astounded.

It must be the boots, he thought. He'd had some like that once, but they'd never done anything so impossible. Or maybe they did, and he just couldn't remember. He looked down at his metal, bootless feet.

Just before he stepped into the chasm, Levi turned to see Rook looking down hopelessly at his feet. He suddenly realized what was wrong. Rook couldn't cross— he didn't have boots.

The other kids were already moving quickly up the stairs to the other side. Levi paused and looked down the tunnel. Perhaps Rook could go back, he thought. Take another route . . . But then the footsteps of approaching Forgers resounded in the tunnel. No, that route was blocked. The Forgers would be upon them in moments.

Rook lowered his gaze, turning away. "Go on," he said. "Go with your friends. I'll . . . find another way." Rook started to move back toward the tunnel and the oncoming Forgers.

Something about his dejected look tore at Levi's heart. He knew how Rook felt. He knew what it was like to feel condemned. He never wanted anyone to feel that way again.

"Wait," Levi said. He knelt down and pulled off his boots. He knew he was doing something he promised he would never do again, but somehow he knew Ruwach would understand. This wasn't for his own selfish purpose. It was for the sake of someone else.

"No, no, you can't—you'll be caught!" said Rook.

"Put them on, hurry!" Levi said.

The vibrations of the Forgers in the passage made the sludge tremble. They were getting close.

"I'm not putting them back on. So you better take them or we'll both be caught," Levi said. He glanced nervously down the tunnel, where he could make out shadows moving in the darkness.

Reluctantly, Rook took the boots and put them on. Despite the fact that his feet were much bigger and made of metal, the boots fit. He raised a hand to Levi in farewell.

"You have to look straight at that light," Levi said. "Don't look away, whatever you do."

Rook nodded, as if he understood. "Thank you," he said. "I won't forget." He turned and stepped out, stones appearing under his feet as he followed the others to the other side of the chasm.

Levi watched him go, a well opening in his heart, filling with something like happiness.

Then he turned to face the Forgers, raising his arms in the air in surrender.

CHAPTER TWENTY-FOUR

Free Indeed

When Rook reached the other side of the stone stairway, he realized he was no longer standing on the edge of the chasm. Unbelievably, the stairway had deposited him on the wide, white balcony of the castle, where he never thought he would be allowed again. He was home. He saw Levi's friends waiting there. They turned to greet him happily, but then their smiles disappeared when they realized Levi was not with him.

"Where's Levi?" Brianna said, her large eyes searching behind him, as if he was hiding somewhere.

"He—he—gave me his boots," Rook said, his voice coming in short bursts. "I didn't ask him to, he just did it. He told me to go—but the Forgers were coming."

Brianna's eyes grew big and round. Her lip trembled slightly. Then she spun on her heels and ran into Xavier, burying her face in his shirt. Manuel hung his head. Evan sprinted to the edge of the balcony and looked out, hoping he would see Levi somewhere, hoping he managed to escape. But there was no sign of him.

"Levi!" he called out. His voice echoed over the landscape. But there was no answer. *"Levi!"* Silence.

Evan turned away, folding his arms, his eyes downcast. "I don't get it. Why would Ruwach send us in there to get someone out but make us leave someone behind?"

"Is that what I have done?"

The kids spun around to see Ruwach gliding through the shining gate of the castle. Rook knelt before him, his head low to the ground.

"Ruwach, I am yours to command. I deserve only to be your slave. I have failed you. I am nothing. I deserve your judgment—"

"Welcome home, Prince Warrior," Ruwach said. He reached out one of his long arms. The bright, glowing hand appeared, touching Rook on the top of his head. Slowly the metal helmet began to melt, revealing sandy-colored hair, hazel eyes, and a round, ruddy face. A *human* face. He was older than the kids had supposed, but not much older, perhaps mid-twenties, but he looked as if he'd had a hard life.

Rook rose slowly as his metal body continued to peel away from his neck and chest, down his arms and legs. He spread his arms in amazement at his own transformation. He wasn't dressed as a slave anymore. He was wearing his own suit of armor.

"Thank you," he said quietly. He dropped to his knees again, bowing low before Ruwach, who drew his hand back into his robe. "Thank you."

Levi's boots, which had been on Rook's feet, now stood empty. Brianna let go of Xavier and ran to the boots, hugging them against her chest. Ruwach bent over her.

"Why are you crying, Princess?"

"Because they took Levi," she said between hiccups. "He gave Rook his boots and now he's a prisoner—"

"Do you not believe the Words I gave to you?"

"Gave to me?"

"To all of you."

Brianna looked down at her breastplate—the orb was spinning, churning out words that floated into the air above them.

Once freed, always free.

"I don't understand," Brianna said, shaking her head. "How can that be true?"

"It is true always. Even for those who seem not to know it."

"But Levi knew it, didn't he?"

Ruwach's head nodded once. "Indeed he did."

Just then the sound of a terribly out-of-tune trumpet blasted the air, followed by the irregular thump of beating wings. The kids and Rook turned, dumfounded, to see Tannyn the dragon coming in for a landing in the courtyard. They scattered quickly as he crash-landed on his belly, his giant wings flapping crazily, bellowing another trumpet call that made them cover their ears and shut their eyes.

Tannyn skidded to a stop inches from the castle gate. The kids opened their eyes, staring at the huge creature in confusion. What was Tannyn doing here? Ruwach hadn't summoned him, although Ruwach seemed unsurprised by his arrival. He moved toward the dragon and nodded his hooded head slowly. Tannyn nodded back, panting like a dog and lowering his head to the ground as if he wanted to be petted.

Brianna, despite her sorrow, ran up to pat Tannyn's head. And when she did, she caught a movement and turned her head to see something—*someone*—sliding down the dragon's long, scaly neck.

It was Levi.

"Levi!" Brianna ran to her best friend, throwing her arms around him in a huge hug as he landed on his bare feet. She couldn't say anything else for a long time. Just hugged him tight.

"I can't breathe," Levi said, laughing.

The boys ran up to him, patting his back and cheering. Rook and Ruwach watched their reunion silently.

"What happened?" Brianna asked finally, letting him go. "How did you get free?"

"Not really sure," Levi said, glancing at Ruwach. "I was standing at the edge, and the Forgers were just about to get me. Then I heard this loud noise and saw Tannyn flying into the canyon, zigzagging every which way. So—I jumped."

"Onto his back?" Evan asked. "Cool!"

"Yeah, I guess so," Levi said. "Well, he caught me anyway. And brought me here."

"Once freed, always free," Brianna said, laughing through her tears.

"That's what I kept thinking about. I figured, if it were true, then they couldn't hold me. I didn't know how it was going to work out, but at least I knew that."

"Have you forgotten something, Warrior?" said Ruwach slyly, raising one robed arm to indicate the empty pair of boots. Levi nodded, walked over to the boots, and put them on his own feet again.

"Hey, Ru," said Evan, ignoring Xavier's scowl at the name, "you know, I was thinking, it would be sort of nice if we had a way to . . . to . . . get instructions from The Book back home, like when we need help with stuff."

Ruwach's head nodded once. "You can. You must."

"We can?" said Brianna. "How?"

"It's at the tip of your finger."

"What does that mean?" said Evan. But as usual, Ruwach didn't explain. Instead, he motioned to the large entry doors.

"Your feast is waiting—for all of you," Ruwach said, giving a special nod to Rook, who bowed his head in gratitude.

The kids raced each other into the feasting hall—all but Xavier, who hung back, moving to Ruwach. He took the key from his boot and held it up before the guide.

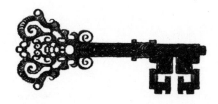

"This opened the prison doors," he said. "I was thinking maybe it was the key that was stolen . . . you know, the one that opens our doors in the Cave."

Ruwach's hood twitched when he saw it.

"It is not that key," said the guide in a sonorous voice. "But it is a key."

"I know it's a key, but . . ."

"It is a *key* to the key, but it is not the key."

Xavier blinked, totally confused. "Uh, I'm not sure I—"

"You will, soon. May I?" Ruwach reached out with his glowing hand to take the key, and it disappeared quickly up his sleeve. "Well done, Prince Xavier."

"It was Manuel who found it," Xavier said.

Ruwach's head nodded knowingly. "It is good you went back for him then, isn't it?"

"Yeah. Guess so." Xavier turned to go back into the feasting hall, but then paused, looking back at Ruwach. "Will we *ever* get to see what's in those rooms?"

"When that time comes, it will be your choice, not mine," Ruwach said. With that, the little guide spun around and sped away, and Xavier found himself wrapped in clouds and light.

CHAPTER TWENTY-FIVE

The Power of the Shoes

Levi, look alive!" Mr. J. Ar said, passing the ball to his son. Levi was so startled he let the ball bounce off his shoulder. "You okay, son?"

"Yeah, fine," Levi said. He glanced at Xavier, Evan, Brianna, and Manuel. He could tell they were just as confused as he was. They were back on the basketball court, like nothing had ever happened. Just like before.

Levi shook off his confusion and ran after the ball, throwing it back to his father. Mr. J. Ar tossed it to Xavier, who dribbled around expertly before passing the ball to Manuel. Manuel threw the ball wildly as Evan rushed over to block him. The ball, by some miracle, swished through the net.

"You made a basket!" Xavier shouted, retrieving the ball.

"I did?" said Manuel, looking up.

"Hey, Manuel, how did you break your glasses?" asked Mr. J. Ar, coming over to get the ball.

Manuel stared at Mr. J. Ar a moment, then took off his glasses and looked at them. He couldn't see them very well, so he rubbed his finger across the lenses— and felt a big crack. He held up the glasses to show the other kids—it was proof that everything they'd been through had been real. They grinned at each other. Manuel turned back to Mr. J. Ar.

"Uh—must be the humidity," he said. "Sudden changes in atmospheric pressure can cause glass to crack."

"Sudden changes?" Mr. J. Ar said. He raised an eyebrow, gazing at the other kids knowingly. "Oh, I see."

Xavier was about to pass the ball to Levi when Landon shuffled over to the court, his hands deep in his pockets. He glared at them meaningfully before slumping onto the bench, his elbows resting on spread knees. He kept staring.

Trying to ignore Landon, Xavier threw the ball to Levi, who dribbled it toward the basket. Evan came in to block him. Levi glanced over at Manuel, who stood frozen like a statue, poised to run if necessary.

Then, for some strange reason, while watching Landon out of the corner of his eye, Levi thought of Rook. Something about them seemed similar.

The prisoner had been bound helplessly in his cell, chained up behind iron bars. Levi thought of the tears that had made rust stains down his cheek. He felt his stomach do a little twist, just like it did before a big test or a super hard skateboarding trick. Instead of dribbling the ball, he held onto it and walked over to where Landon was sitting.

Landon looked up at him, and Levi again had the sense of something familiar. Landon's eyes, despite their insolence, held a hint of weariness, and of hope. Just like Rook's had. Levi knew then what he needed to do.

"You wanna play?" he said quietly. He offered the ball.

Landon's eyes widened. He straightened, looking from Levi to the ball and back again. None of the other kids made a sound. Levi supposed they were all just staring at him, wondering if he had gone nuts.

Landon leaned back, and for a moment Levi thought he was going to take him up on his offer. But then Landon shook his head and stood up, waving Levi off. He started to walk away, his hands once more thrust into the pockets of his baggy jeans.

That's when Levi noticed his shoes. Landon wore old, heavy work boots, so ratty they were held together with duct tape. He couldn't play basketball in those shoes.

"Hold up," Levi said.

Landon turned, waiting silently.

"You can wear my shoes," Levi said. "I mean, if you want to play."

Landon's face changed, the hard scowl softening a little. He glanced down at his feet, and Levi saw that he was actually embarrassed. Levi made up his mind then. He sat down on the bench and took off his shoes. His brand new Vans. Black with the gold swish. He held them a moment, taking one more good look, before offering them to Landon.

Landon looked at Levi as if he'd lost his mind. The other kids exchanged surprised looks. Mr. J. Ar smiled to himself.

Landon shuffled back over to the bench and sat down. "Why you giving me your shoes?"

"So you can play."

"But then *you* can't play."

Levi shrugged. "That's okay. I'll just watch. I'm not that good at basketball anyway. You're probably better than me."

"How you know that?"

"Saw you playing once, awhile ago." Levi remembered leaving the Rec one night, when his dad was locking up, and seeing Landon dribbling the ball around the basketball court when he thought no one was watching.

Landon shifted around, glancing up at the kids staring at him. Then he looked back at Levi. He reached over and took the shoes from Levi's outstretched hands. "Thanks," he murmured.

"No problem," Levi said.

Landon laced up the shoes as Levi watched, then picked up the ball and walked out onto the court. Manuel stood in frozen terror near the basket, perhaps imagining that Landon would use the first opportunity he had to pulverize him. Landon bounced the ball once, twice. He started to dribble. Xavier ran in to block him, but Landon evaded him easily—he was quick for a kid his size. He spun, bounced the ball, headed for a layup. But he stopped in midjump and seemed to notice Manuel cowering under the basket. For a long moment it looked as though Landon really would pummel the kid with the glasses. He seemed to think about it. Then, almost gently, he bounced the ball over to Manuel.

Manuel caught it, shocked. He hesitated, not sure what he was supposed to do. Then in desperation he threw the ball up to the basket and missed. He winced, leaning backward, preparing himself for retaliation.

Landon didn't seem to notice. He retrieved the ball and kept on playing.

Levi sat on the bench watching, barefoot once again. But this time, he wasn't sad. His heart was full of something wonderful, something no skateboard trick or basketball score could ever give him. He saw his dad looking at him and smiled broadly. His dad smiled back.

Brianna came to sit down by Levi. She glanced down at his bare feet.

"You and shoes," she said, putting on some lip gloss. "You just can't keep them on your feet, can you?"

Levi looked over at her and smiled.

"Guess not."

Brianna's phone chirped. She pulled it out of her hoodie pocket, surprised it was actually there. She unlocked it, and the app called *UNSEEN* opened immediately.

"Hey, look," she said, showing it to Levi. "The app opened."

"Yeah, but it's the same weird pictures and symbols," Levi said.

Brianna thought for a minute. "Remember what Ruwach said? The Book was at the tip of our fingers. Remember? Maybe this is what he meant—that this app is like a *portable* Book."

"I thought that was one of his weird expressions."

"Well, maybe it isn't. Maybe it's something else." Brianna placed her index finger on the phone and held it there for several seconds. All at once, the pictures and symbols began moving around the page, reorganizing into something they both recognized: The Crest of Ahoratos. "It's the Crest!"

"It's the cover of The Book," Levi said. "Open it!"

Brianna touched the screen, and the image flipped open to reveal a blank page with a blinking cursor. Brianna touched the line, unsure of what do at first. Then she did the only thing she could think to: she typed her name. Instantly more words appeared on the page.

Well done, good and faithful servant. You have shown you can be trusted with a small thing. You will be trusted with something bigger.

Levi pulled his own phone out of his pocket and opened the app. He put his finger on the screen and heard a metallic clink—he remembered then that the tip of his finger was metal. He pulled back his hand and rubbed his thumb over the cold surface. His heart sank.

Brianna put a hand on his shoulder. "Why don't you try your other hand?" she said gently.

Levi shifted the phone to his right hand and tried again with his left index finger. The app responded. The image of The Book appeared, just as it had for Brianna. He breathed a sigh of relief.

He typed in his name, and the same instruction Brianna had gotten appeared on his phone as well. He stared at it a long moment—after all that had transpired, he never thought he would see those words written to him. He looked at Brianna and grinned.

"It says we'll be trusted with something bigger," he said. "So I guess . . . we'll be going back."

Brianna nodded, the corner of her mouth turning up in a smile.

"Stellar."

Epilogue

Ruwach moved through the silent halls of the Cave, toward the room with the empty box. Rook followed more slowly, gazing around him at this place he had not been for so long—a place he thought he would never be again. It was a miracle, he thought, that he was back in the Cave. That Ruwach had allowed him to come back.

He watched Ruwach's white glowing hand emerge from the long sleeve—it contained the key Xavier had given him. The key that had opened Rook's prison door.

"What will you do with it?" he asked the guide.

"You will keep it safe." Ruwach held the key out to Rook.

"Me?" Rook hung back, not wanting to touch it. "No . . ."

"Yes, this is your mission now. To protect this key. Make sure it does not fall back into Ponéros's hands."

"He has plenty more prison keys," Rook said.

"Yes, but every one we wrest from him—is a victory."

After a moment Rook reached out and took the key. He placed it in his pocket.

"You know Ponéros will be angry when he realizes I'm gone," he said.

"He knows already," Ruwach said. "We must prepare the warriors. Ponéros suffered a defeat today. He will . . . retaliate."

"Have you told James?"

"Yes. He will watch over them. As will we."

Rook nodded. "But the key . . . the one that opens the doors to the warriors' rooms . . . do you want me to go back and get it? Because I will, you know. I owe you that."

Ruwach shook his hooded head slowly. "You have done enough. I will do the rest." The hand withdrew. "Go in peace, Prince Rook. I will call for you when I need you again."

Rook smiled and turned away, glancing down one of the dark tunnels. He could just see the outline of one of the locked doors. He felt a pang of longing—he still did not know what was in them. Why hadn't he opened his door when he had first stolen the key? At the time he hadn't cared—he could think of nothing but the glorious riches Ponéros had promised him. It had never occurred to him to wonder why Ponéros was so determined to have the key. And now, it was probably lost for good.

He glanced back and realized Ruwach was no longer there. He was alone in the room, with the empty box. He took a deep breath, putting his hand inside his pocket to feel the prison key. *Keep it safe,* Ruwach had commanded. And he would. But he would also use it. Because there were many other prisoners who needed to be set free.

"Thank you," he whispered, into the air. He reached over and closed the empty box. And then he turned and left the empty room.

To discover the
hidden secrets of The Prince Warriors, go to

www.theprincewarriors.com

FROM *NEW YORK TIMES* BEST-SELLING AUTHOR

PRISCILLA SHIRER

with GINA DETWILER

THE PRINCE WARRIORS AND THE UNSEEN INVASION

Keep reading for a sneak peek at book 2 . . .

The Prince Warriors and the Unseen Invasion

Rook knew that things were not going according to plan.

He jumped from beam to beam, pulling his companion along with him, the prisoner he'd just released. "Hurry!" he whisper-shouted, although he knew no amount of coaxing would help. The prisoner's legs were encased in metal, the joints stiff from disuse. His arms were still flesh, however, which made it somewhat easier for Rook to keep a grip on him.

"I can't," the prisoner panted. "I . . . need . . . to . . . stop . . ."

Rook paused to let him rest, balanced precariously on a narrow girder that hung across a stretch of empty space. Below them lay a black abyss. Above them the maze of steel girders wound upward in a twisted skeleton, blocking out most of the churning, red sky.

It sickened him to be back in the Fortress of Chaós again—the dark castle at the edge of Skot'os, the lair of the enemy, Ponéros. Rook had escaped from this place not long before, rescued by a group of kids who had brought him a message: *Once freed, always free.* He'd returned to bring that message to another prisoner. He'd also brought the key.

The key.

It opened the prison doors. The kids had taken it from the enemy. Rook reached into his pocket, fingering the long shining object with the scrolled handle, making sure it was still there. He couldn't lose it, whatever happened.

"This way." He beckoned to his companion, urging him to follow along the beam. Rook's boots gripped the steel girder like rubber, giving him assurance he wouldn't slip. But the prisoner's metal feet scraped eerily, making Rook's hair stand on end. He remembered all too well what it felt like to hobble along on metal feet, now restored to flesh, thanks to those kids. And to Ruwach, the one who had sent them.

If only I had thought this through a little more, Rook mused to himself. Getting into the fortress had been easy, *too* easy. The narrow beam of light from his breastplate had lit up his path with each step. No one tried to stop him. The Forgers—the fully mechanized soldiers of Ponéros's evil army—were nowhere in sight. Yet Rook had had the feeling he was being watched. The Ents, perhaps, those nasty metal bugs that liked to pass themselves off as butterflies. They'd probably been tracking him with their red laser eyes, unseen.

Rook should have known better than to simply go out the same way he'd gone in. But he was so determined to free a soul and get out of that horrible place as soon as he could that he hadn't taken proper precautions. He thought he knew the way. But the fortress seemed to have shifted around him, morphed—his path wiped away, every exit he had known blocked.

Chaos. Confusion. *That* was Ponéros's security system.

The beam under them shuddered, forcing them to stop. Loud booms filled the air around them, the sound of heavy footsteps echoing through the maze of girders.

"It's them," said the prisoner in a squeaky, pathetic voice. "They're coming now."

Forgers, Rook thought. They had trapped him. Now they would come to retake him and the prisoner both.

"What's your name?" Rook asked.

"It's . . . F-f-finn," stuttered the prisoner.

"Well, Finn, we have to get to the end of this beam. And then . . . we'll figure something out." Rook hoped his voice didn't sound as hopeless as he felt. He inched his way along the slender path, keeping one hand on Finn's arm so he wouldn't lose his balance and tumble into the abyss below them.

After what seemed like forever, he got to the end of the girder and grabbed a vertical beam that projected from the empty space below. Finn grabbed on as well. The whole structure trembled and shook with the sound of approaching Forgers. Red, round glowing orbs appeared in the inky blackness around them, closing in.

"Which way?" whispered Finn.

"Up here!"

A voice seemed to come from the sky. A young voice. A *girl's* voice.

Both Rook and Finn looked up, straining to see who had spoken. They couldn't really see anything except small angular blotches of red sky peeking through the grid of beams overhead and . . . stars. A spray of minuscule lights seemed to be pouring in from the tangled web of girders above them. Not stars . . . *Sparks*, those tiny, brilliant balls of light that dwelled in the

Cave. Rook felt a well of relief open in his soul. *Ruwach had come!* But the voice was not Ruwach's. It definitely belonged to a young girl.

"Come *on*, will you?" the girl's voice scolded him. He could just barely see the outline of a human standing on a girder, silhouetted by fragments of the churning red sky.

"This way! Climb!"

How in the world did that human—a girl—get all the way up there? Maybe it was a trick. Ponéros was good at tricks. Deception was his game.

Yet what choice did he have but to follow? A deep, unexplainable assurance settled over him, a rooted calm.

Rook turned to Finn, whose half-human face stared back at him, fear rolling in his eyes. "Did you see that?"

A huge Forger vaulted onto the girder they'd just crossed, its metal fists closed and ready to strike. As the Forger lunged for him, Rook drew his sword and swung, slicing off one of its metal arms. The Forger bellowed, its red eyes spinning with rage as the severed mechanical arm broke apart and turned to dust. It stumbled backward and fell from the beam to the dark void below. But soon there was another one to take its place. And another.

"Great," Rook muttered to himself.

"You coming or what?" said the voice above him.

"How am I supposed to . . . ?"

"Use your belt!"

The belt!

Rook suddenly understood. As the second Forger charged forward, Rook took off his belt—a wide, plain white belt that had no visible clasp. He tossed one end upward. It stretched out to several times its own length, the end wrapping snugly around a beam above. The belt, stretched thin, began to hum like a tightly wound guitar string. "Hold on to me!" Rook said and jumped, his boots launching him and the prisoner into the air, as more Forgers converged under them. Rook swung one leg over the beam on which his belt was wrapped, hauling himself and Finn over the top.

"Piece of cake," he said breathlessly, giving Finn a little encouraging smile. Finn tried to smile back with his half-metal face.

"You're too slow!" said the girl, who had scrambled up to an even higher perch.

That girl was starting to get on Rook's nerves.

Rook looked down and saw the Forgers climbing up the steel girders toward him. *Pretty nimble,* he thought, *for big, hulking hardware.* He unwrapped his belt, threw one end up to yet another beam and jumped again, holding tightly onto Finn.

Rook could see the girl more clearly now. She had scrambled up toward the top of the fortress, where bare beams thrust into the swirling, red-purple sky. Her fiery red hair whipped around her face in the biting wind. She held on with one hand, glancing out over the expanse of sky.

"Come *on*, already!"

Rook jumped again, Finn clinging to him, the belt propelling them ever upward. Below them Forgers continued to gather, scaling the beams, their red eyes piercing the darkness. Where on earth was that girl going? She seemed to be leading him into a trap.

When finally Rook and his half-human charge made it to the pinnacle, the little girl with red hair greeted them with a big sigh.

"Took you long enough," she snipped.

"Hey, you try dragging up a two-hundred pound hunk of metal—no offense." Rook glanced at Finn in apology then turned back to the girl. He unwrapped his belt and refastened it around his waist, making sure his sword was still secure. The girl, he noticed, didn't have a sword, only a belt, breastplate and boots. Like those other kids, he remembered. The ones who had rescued him. But this girl hadn't been with them, he was pretty sure. Again, he wondered if this was a trap—if this girl were working for Ponéros himself.

"Who are you, by the way? Did Ruwach send you? How are we getting out of here?"

"We're going to jump, of course!"

"What?" Rook blinked, hoping he'd heard her wrong. The beam on which they were perched shook with the vibrations of the Forgers clambering toward them.

"Now!" the girl said, with something like glee. "Let's go!"

Before he had time to react, she'd grabbed his arm and jumped straight into the turbulent sky, taking Rook and Finn with her.

Acknowledgments

Jerry Shirer Sr.—Thank you for being a man's man; fearing God, honoring your family, and giving our sons—Jackson, Jerry Jr., and Jude—a compass that points the way to godly manhood. I'm forever grateful that you made me your wife and now a mother of sons. I'm asking God to make our three boys into Prince Warriors just like you.

Jerry Jr. and Jude—Don't panic. This series is a trilogy. The next two books are already dedicated to each of you. Your momma loves you. Your father and I are so honored that we get to raise such strong and courageous Prince Warriors as you.

Kit and Caleb—You are genius. I could have never imagined that the little boys I've watched grow from newborns to curious toddlers and then creative and inspired teenagers would teach me so much. You are unbelievably intelligent, innovative, and profound young men. The insight you have added to this series is invaluable. I pray that no matter how old you get, neither of you will ever lose your brilliant imaginations. Continue to cultivate your individuality. Fitting in is overrated. YOU are the epitome of Prince Warriors.

Gina—This book and this series could not have come to fruition without you. Your pen is a fine-tuned instrument, turning ordinary concepts into fantastical landscapes and unforgettable scenes. Thank you for being my partner—for taking characters and storylines that I've had tucked in my mind and unorganized computer files for years and making them come to life. You, my friend, are an answer to prayer.

Dan, Jana, Michelle, Rachel, and the B&H Kids publishing group—Thank you for catching my vision and running alongside me to see it through to the end. Jerry and I are so honored to serve the next generation of warriors with you.

To my nieces and nephews, Kariss, Jessica, Tre', Kanaan, Joel, J2, Kamden, Kelsey, Kylar, Alena, Kaity, Camryn, and Olivia—You were the inspiration behind these characters. And with every page written, I asked God to make each of you courageous and faithful Prince/Princess Warriors. May the enemy shake in his boots when he sees the fire of God's Spirit in you. The legacy of our family lives on with you.

About the Authors

Priscilla Shirer is a homemade cinnamon-roll baker, Bible teacher, and best-selling author who didn't know her books (*The Resolution for Women* and *Fervent*) were on *The New York Times* Best Seller list until somebody else told her. Because who has time to check such things while raising three rapidly growing sons? When she and Jerry, her husband of sixteen years, are not busy leading *Going Beyond Ministries*, they spend most of their time cleaning up after and trying to satisfy the appetites of these guys. And that is what first drove Priscilla to dream up this fictional story about the very un-fictional topic of spiritual warfare—to help raise up a new generation of Prince Warriors under her roof. And under yours.

Gina Detwiler was planning to be a teacher but switched to writing so she wouldn't have to get up so early in the morning. She's written a couple of books in various genres (*Avalon* and *Hammer of God*, under the name Gina Miani) and dramas published by Lillenas and DramaMinistry, but she prefers writing (and reading) books for young people. She lives in Buffalo, New York, where it snows a lot, with her husband and three beautiful daughters. She is honored and grateful to be able to work with Priscilla on *The Prince Warriors*.

Visit
THEPRINCEWARRIORS.COM
to find out more about

UNSEEN: *The Prince Warriors App,*

UNSEEN: *The Prince Warriors 365 Devotional,*

and book 2 in the trilogy—
The Prince Warriors and the Unseen Invasion.

Every WORD Matters
BHPublishingGroup.com